The Best Erotic Short Stories of 2024

Featuring Rough Sex, Gangbangs, Anal, Threesomes, Cuckold, Age Gap, Daddies, BDSM, and more...

Rayna Russell

GO Publishing LLC

Contents

Introduction

Hello dear friends,

Another year... another anthology of the best erotic short stories!

If we haven't met, my name is Rayna Russell, and I'm a writer, editor, and (most importantly) a lover of fantastically written smut.

Each year, I collect short stories from my favorite writers and publish them in a volume for you to enjoy.

I've listened to your feedback and made a few changes. For example, I got some really enthusiastic emails from readers who appreciated the stories written by men, so I sought out some new male writers. This volume also includes more writers of color, and I think their steamy contributions really make this year's anthology special.

If you're listening to the audiobook, you'll notice that there are several voices, suited to the individual stories. That really makes the experience richer for listeners.

As always, I love to hear from you! If you have any thoughts or suggestions, or if you want more information on any particular writer, reach out! raynarussellerotica@gmail.com

As ever, I'm wildly appreciative that you're choosing to spend your time with me. I thank you, and I love you.

Your friend,

Rayna

Chapter 1

Journal

by Janine Kemp

My mom told me that I was far too young to be having an existential crisis. I get why she said that, but if I disclosed the full reason for my angst, she'd be even more worried about me. My mom and my closest friends all say that I'm an old soul. Maybe that's why the things that seem to get them excited about life just fall flat for me. I'm not crazy about social media. It just feels like a time suck to me. I don't like bingeing the shows that they like to binge. I don't like the bar scene...or the club scene, for that matter. In fact, I'm not entirely sure what it is that I *do* like. Other than my boyfriend, Eli. My relationship with Eli is just... different. My friends have yet to be in a committed relationship, so I'm a little wary to talk to them about what we do. On a whim, I decided to buy a journal. Don't all the cool, creative girls write in journals? I decided to splurge a little and got a beautiful leather-bound notebook with a gold floral inlay.

Dear Diary - Monday

Today I was at work when I saw Marianne approaching me with a smirk. I was sure that she had some juicy gossip from the weekend that she wanted to share with me. I was trying to decide whether or not I was in the mood to hear it when she practically sprinted over to me, covering her mouth with her hand. My interest was piqued. Maybe I would be interested in what she had to tell me. She scream-whispered to me that she didn't know I had a boyfriend... or girlfriend, she said with a wink.

"Um yeah... I've had one for about 3 months. Why?"

"BeCAUSE! Your neck...You naughty little girl!"

I reflexively reached up to touch my neck while I frowned at Marianne to discourage her giggling.

"I've gotta get to work, girl. See you later?" I said to her, and then I promptly went to the ladies' room to discover that she wasn't exaggerating. I don't know how I showered, put on makeup, and got dressed for work without

noticing it. A hickey. Right there in the most sensitive part of my neck. I know I love it when Eli kisses me there, and I sometimes lose myself when I feel his tongue tentatively exploring, but I had no idea he'd left a mark. I grabbed my foundation and did the best I could to cover it while smiling to myself. I better go text Eli and let him know that he's in trouble.

Dear Diary – Tuesday

Poor Eli! He felt so bad about the hickey. I wasn't mad at him, though. He told me that he had a hard time controlling himself around me.

He said that I turn him into a wild animal!

It felt so powerful to think of myself as this seductress. I always assumed my power lay in being submissive. The couple of guys that I had been with in the past seemed to really get off on taking control of me, which was sort of what happened with Eli last night. But this was different. He had this helpless look in his eyes...as if he really couldn't control himself with me. The more aggressive I was, the harder he breathed.

"That's right... just like that, baby," I told him. I had never really talked dirty before. I was more of a whim-

perer. But last night... I don't know. I looked Eli in the eyes while he was on top of me. I licked my lips and hoisted myself on top of him. Eli had at least 60 pounds on me, so it wasn't easy. But once I straddled him and pinned his hands back over his head, the look in eyes made me feel like the most powerful woman in the world. I decided to give him a taste of his own medicine. I bent down and gently bit his earlobe. I felt his body relax beneath me. He liked it. I kissed him behind the ear, inhaling the woodsy scent of his cologne. God, he always smells so good! I licked him right in the same spot that he gave me a hickey in. His moan made something twinge deep inside me. I felt lightheaded. I bit him softly and he pulled his hands free then, grabbing me. He stuck his hands in my hair and grinded his hips under mine as he continued to moan. He was so turned on! I was making him feel that way? I bit him harder and sucked. Although Eli is darker than me, I knew that he would have a mark of his own to explain. For some reason, the thought of that really, really turned me on. But I didn't have much time to think about what to do next because Eli suddenly flipped me around. No. 'Flipped' isn't quite the way to describe it. He sort of body-slammed me and ended up with his hand around my throat. The breath was knocked out of me, and I gasped in surprise. What the hell? Eli's eyes went wide as he seemed to *realize how rough he had been. He released my throat as I tried to catch my breath. Suddenly he was cradling me and apologizing. He lost control... again. He was so sorry. I told him that he didn't have to apologize. That we were having fun...exploring...experimenting. Eli wasn't buying it. He told me that he had never felt this way before. That I just 'did' something to him. I knew the feeling. How would I explain just how wet this whole thing had made me?*

"So what are you saying?" Eli pulled the lettuce, tomato, and cucumber out of my refrigerator for our salad.

I flipped over the chicken breast I was sautéing. "I'm saying that you don't have to keep apologizing. I'm not mad."

Eli stopped and looked at me, squinting a bit. "Okay. If you're not *mad*, then what are you?"

"I'm... I don't know. I'm...turned on?"

"Are you asking me or telling me?"

I smiled my new confident smile at him. "I'm fucking turned on. Okay?"

I watched Eli's face as he processed at least five different emotions. "Is this a trick?"

I raised an eyebrow at him. "Trick?"

"Yeah. Are you trying to get me to admit something and then you're gonna be all grossed out or something?"

"Why do you think I'm trying to trick you?" I asked. "Did you not notice how...wet I was?" I said shyly.

"I mean...I'm not gonna lie. You were soooo wet. I just... I wasn't sure. I never wanna hurt you."

"You didn't!" I interjected.

"Okay...so... you liked it? You like it...rough?"

"I think I do. So...stop apologizing," I said coyly.

"In that case," Eli said with an evil glint in his eye, "try to give me another hickey and I'm gonna have to spank you...bad girl."

Dear Diary – Wednesday

Eli used his key, just like I asked him to. I was showered, wearing one of his T-shirts with just panties underneath. He walked in just as I was about to fix myself a drink. I held up a glass and raised an eyebrow. He nodded as I made two gin and tonics with extra lime.

I started my playlist as we sipped our drinks, sort of feeling each other out. How would this night proceed? I had admitted to Eli that I wasn't turned off when he got rough with me. And not only that, I was into it. What will he do with that information?

I didn't have to wait long to find out. I decided to take charge again. I took a big sip of my drink just as the playlist hit my current favorite song.

> Know you got it coming, babe
> You took this shit from zero to a hundred, babe
> I hope you finally get it on your judgment day
> 'Cause you're gonna pay, babe, you're gonna pay, babe

I came up behind Eli and put my hands around his waist, singing the lyrics into his ear. He continued standing there sipping his drink. It almost felt like he was holding his breath. I slid my hands up from his waist and over his chest to feel his nipples harden through his shirt. Guess guys' nipples work the same as girls'...

I pinched his nipples hard and heard his sharp inhale. I slid my hands down from his chest, over his rigid abs to *something that was even harder. Wow, he was practically throbbing in my hand! I gave him a squeeze and heard him suck his breath in once again. He tilted his head back slightly as I circled around him and came to stand right in front him. I looked up at him seductively while removing the clip from my hair and gently pressing my body into his. We swayed slightly to the music, and I began to feel lightheaded again. That was a new sensation for me. Was this what it felt like to be completely turned on? NOT in my head for once, but fully present in this moment, wanting nothing more than to be ravished...or maybe even ravaged by my man?*

Eli sat his drink down hard on the counter and swept me up in one gesture. He picked me up and put me on the counter and before I could say a word, then he pushed me back and snatched my legs apart. He looked up at me as his face hovered between my legs. I've never seen that particular look in his eyes. Eli pulled my legs even farther apart, making a low growling sound as he did. I panicked slightly as his hands tightened around my thighs. He suddenly grabbed me and snatched me to the very edge of the counter. I had a thought that this position reminded me of being at the gynecologist, but before I could fully think anything, Eli bit my thigh so close to where I really wanted him to bite that I screamed/moaned in surprise and frustration. Eli smiled up at me and bit the other thigh. Hard. This time the stockings ripped. I don't know what it was about the sound of them tearing, but I lost it. Eli didn't miss a beat and ripped them apart with his teeth and gnawed his way to my wet center. I gripped the sides of the counter as he sucked my thigh so hard that I knew it would leave a mark. It hurt. I was about to push his head away when he grabbed my right hand and then my left. He pinned them over my head and took his other hand and slid his middle finger into me. I felt my pussy grip his finger like its life depended on it. Eli felt it too and looked up at me.

"Damn" was all he got out. He moved his finger in and out, back and forth. Just as I almost caught my breath (was this really just his finger!?), he slid in another. It felt so good I could barely take it. I felt like I had to... what? Go to the bathroom? But no. This was different. I tensed up and reached for Eli's shoulders. Eli had other ideas. He pushed my hands away and swept me off the counter. I'm not necessarily heavy, but I am tall. I had never experienced anyone handling me with such ease. He picked me up as if I was light as a feather and tossed me onto the couch. I instinctively made myself comfortable, thinking Eli was about to finally put me out of my misery. I wanted him so bad, I could taste it.

Eli straddled me and looked down at me with a wicked gleam in his eye. He asked me if I remembered trying to give him a hickey even after he threatened me with a spanking. I smirked, wondering what he was getting at. He wiped that smile right off my face when he grabbed my shoulder and hip and turned me over – face down. I heard his belt buckle and then I felt his belt. I yelped out of surprise and then pain. That hurt! I tried to look back at Eli's face, but then he popped me again, right on the fleshy part of my ass, but somehow the pain radiated through my body, and I felt myself contract again. I needed to feel him inside of me. I raised my head once again and felt Eli stretch out on top of me.

"Please," I begged.

"Please what?"

"Please...fuck me."

"You look *tired,*" Marianne said sarcastically.

"What?"

Marianne folded her arms and looked around the breakroom conspiratorially. "I saw your boyfriend pick you up yesterday. He's hot! Sorry, no disrespect, but I can totally understand the hickey situation."

"Marianne," I said as I felt my ears getting hot, "I—"

"Sorry, sorry! I have ADHD and I'm on the spectrum. I'm completely inappropriate. I promise you, I'm working on it," she said in one run-on sentence and scurried off before I could tell her to mind her own effing business. I was glad she walked away. I wasn't completely sure what I would've said to her. The thing was, she was right. I was completely exhausted and sore. So, so sore. Eli's spanking and subsequent love-making session had my entire lower body throbbing like I had lifted weights for hours. I was so wet when Eli finally slid into me that we both knew there was no turning back. He fucked me from the back and then missionary. Then I managed to turn him over and rode him without breaking eye contact like I usually did. I was so caught up in the moment that the urge to pee suddenly exploded into an orgasm I had no idea I was capable of. I felt myself pulsating around Eli's manhood and saw the shocked look on his face when he felt it too. I closed my eyes and rode Eli like I was Beyonce mounting a glittering silver Mustang. The feeling continued to intensify until I realized the strange crying/moaning sound was coming from me, and I exploded again. I opened my eyes to Eli switching us around again. He positioned me on all fours and grabbed my waist. I was so weak, I didn't think I'd be able to remain upright. Eli held on tight and slid into me. It was too much. I was coming again, already. I collapsed onto my stomach, and Eli continued to pound into me, his sweat dripping onto my back.

"That's right. This bad little girl likes it from the back, doesn't she?"

All I could do was moan in response. What the fuck was he doing to me?

"You can't answer me? That's rude," Eli panted hoarsely into my ear. Then he bit my neck, and I came again.

"Who told you you could come again?"

"Eli," I moaned helplessly.

"Mmmm, oh now you wanna talk? It's too late, you're already in trouble."

I barely got two hours of sleep before my alarm went off and I had to drag my bruised and battered body into the shower. I briefly thought of calling in sick, but it felt weird to take the day off because my boyfriend had fucked me senseless the night before. I smiled to myself as I threw the remains of my lunch away. I barely had an appetite lately because I was completely consumed with the new direction my relationship was going in. I saw Kevin from Sales smile at me as I made my way back to my desk. I averted my eyes. Once upon a time, I had thought about accepting Kevin's invitation to lunch because I wasn't quite sure what was happening with Eli. Even though I eventually turned it down, I think he decided he'd hold out hope until hell froze over or something. But not only did I have no interest in lunch or anything with Kevin, I didn't even want to talk to or think about another man. Eli had me...sprung.

It didn't help matters that Eli was always so sweet and nurturing afterward. Even though it was painfully obvious that I was into the rough sex, he had made it a point to talk to me about everything and make sure that we were on the same page. And then he would run a bath for me with this special salve he bought and a glass of champagne. After that, he would tenderly massage all of my sore spots as he lotioned my body. This inevitably would get me worked up again. Rinse... repeat.

Thursday, Eli showed up to my job. I had planned on taking the train, but there he was when I stepped off of the elevator. I don't know why, but I pretended not to know him and kept walking, much to Marianne's confusion. Eli followed me until I dipped into a bar at the end of the block. I headed straight to the back and into the bathroom. I walked in with Eli on my heels, and he locked the door behind us. Without making a sound, he reached under my skirt and tore my thong away. I was so glad I'd worn the cheap, flimsy one. He surprised me my putting the ragged fabric in my mouth, and before I could protest, I found myself biting down on it to stifle my scream as Eli pushed me up against the wall and took me from behind. After a few strokes, I pulled myself out of his grasp and pushed him up against the wall. I was going to get that hickey on his neck once and for all. It was only fair. What was this? *Was* I a bad girl? Why was I so wet?! And about to come...again.

Dear Journal – Friday

Eli here. Well, I guess you already know that. Jordana's journaling has had a profound impact on our sex life. I've got so much going on in my head, I thought I'd get it out on paper. Where to begin. This girl! So innocent looking. So pretty and pure. I never thought in a million years that I could have the girl of my dreams and live out my sexual fantasies at the same time. She's so fucking hot. I can't believe we did that in the bar that she and her coworkers go to. That's the only way she was able to distract me enough to get to my neck. She walked right past the bartender that knows all of us by name...right past the waitress that works every Friday. Of course, I had to follow. I couldn't back down. Not after allll the shit I had been talking. I followed Jordana into the bathroom and let instinct take over. I took her from the back while she clawed at the wall with her panties stuffed into her mouth. To date, she has not used our safe word, so I didn't let up. I fucked her until I almost had an asthma attack. I knew someone could be knocking on the door any second, and I needed her to come first. But I ended up coming first, so hard that I felt like my knees would buckle, and then Jordana switched it up on me by pulling me out of her, putting me in her mouth and swallowing. SWALLOWING! If I hadn't been so surprised, there was no way she would've finally got that hickey on my neck.

Chapter 2

The Christmas Present

by Casey Wisniewski

"Are you just gonna stare at my ass and not help me with this?" Jen asked, breaking my concentration.

"Baby, I told you that I would do that *for* you once I finish this PowerPoint for class," I said.

"Okay, I'll leave the boxes for later," Jen said, grabbing her cell phone out of her pocket. She came over to where I was, pushed my laptop aside, and straddled me. "But we do need to discuss Jamaica."

We had decided to visit Jamaica for New Year's Eve. Jen's aunt and uncle still lived there, so we could have a great vacation and also spend time with two of our favorite people.

"What do we need to discuss?"

"So," Jen said, pulling up her calendar app, "we're pretty much all set for the trip, but things are gonna be tight til then," she said.

I slid my hands up the sides of her smooth thighs. "Tell me something I don't know, pretty lady."

"Well, I say all that to say that I don't think we should get each other anything for Christmas. I *know* my baby loves me. You have nothing to prove. Let's just skip it."

"I hear what you're saying, baby. But there's no way I'm not gonna do something for you for Christmas."

Jen tapped her chin, thinking. "Okay, let's do something, but maybe just make it about the experience and not gifts."

"Not those coupons again..." I said, remembering our first year of dating when we made coupons for massages, extended kisses, foot rubs, and every manner of thing.

"No! Not the coupons," Jen said laughing. "But maybe an elevated experience. We could drive somewhere and sightsee or something."

"Okay! I like where you're going with this. As a matter of fact, I'm thinking...what about New York? I'll handle everything. It'll be a perfect day. We could go see the lights on 5th Avenue, go to the Rockefeller Center, eat a pretzel in Central Park; have the perfect tourist experience."

"New York City?" Jen said, and I could see the wheels turning in her mind.

"Yes, that's the one," I joked. "It's only about a three-hour drive. It'll be fun."

"Hmmm, okay," Jen said, her smile widening. "I like it! We could see Monica."

"Yep, we could see Monica. Maybe do a Thursday through Sunday type thing? What do you think?"

Jen smiled and put her arms around my neck. "I think I *love* that idea. Maybe we could stay at a cool Airbnb and live like the locals. You know, we could walk to Joe's hotdog stand and Bob's old-school deli and Lou's famous bagel shop!"

I frowned. "Are Joe, Bob, and Lou actual people that you know?"

Jen scooted farther up on my lap and placed a kiss on my neck. "Nope, but you get the idea, right?"

"Yes, baby. I get it. We'll have an amazing time," I said distractedly as I began to unbutton my wife's blouse.

"Hey, where's your coupon?" she said, laughing.

"It's in the mail," I told her as I unfastened her bra to release my other two favorite girls.

"You really thought of everything," Jen said as she bit into her pretzel.

"Well, you found that amazing Airbnb," I told her. "I may never want to stay in a hotel again."

Jen looked at me with a gleam in her eye. "Well, 5th Avenue was simply amazing, and we had our pretzel... I think we should head back to the apartment."

"Already? I thought you wanted to stop at that bookstore you were telling me about. We can Uber there in like 20 minutes."

"Yeah..." she said slowly. "I was thinking we could save that until tomorrow."

"But what about dinner?" I asked, confused, hoping that Jen wasn't feeling unwell. "You feeling okay?"

Jen flashed her radiant smile. "I am fine, baby. I just have a little surprise for you."

"Okay...so you *don't* want to go to dinner? But Monica's meeting us there, right? Should I call and cancel the reservation?"

"I already took care of all that. Please, no more questions. Okay?"

When we got back to the apartment, I unlocked the door and almost jumped out of my shoes. Monica was standing in the living room.

"Finally!" she said.

I looked from her to Jen, who didn't seem at all surprised. "Uh, Monica? How did you get in here... Wait, what are you doing here?"

"Surprise!" They both said in unison.

I just shook my head, waiting for an explanation. I was happy to see our friend but clearly not as excited as they were. There was an awkward moment of silence before Jen said, "Baby, look at her legs. Aren't they pretty?"

Bemused, I smiled as we removed our coats and boots. "Are we about to set Monica up? I thought you swore off of playing matchmaker."

"Baby, *look* at her."

I looked at Monica, who was standing there smiling at me. I had about a hundred thoughts go through my head simultaneously. Was this a trick? Of course, I had noticed Monica's legs long ago and just about everything else about her. While Jen was tall and light-skinned with an athletic build and an amazing ass, Monica was voluptuous. She was shorter, with a milk chocolate complexion and honestly did have the nicest legs I had ever seen. Jen's breasts were small and bite-sized, just the way I liked them. But Monica's breasts were about three times the size of Jen's. She looked soft and sensuous. And Monica wore her dark hair long and straight where Jen kept her sandy hair in its curly state.

"Baby?" Jen was saying. "Are you okay?"

"I'm fine," I said. "But what is happening right now? What are you guys up to?"

"Okay, I'll spell it out for you," Jen said, clapping her hands like a little kid. "We're exchanging experiences, right? Well, this is what I got for you."

"What?" I said, still wondering what the hell was going on.

Jen walked over to Monica and tucked a strand of hair behind Monica's ear as they continued smiling at each other. I felt my jeans tighten in a way that I didn't need my wife's best friend to notice. However, they took a step closer to each other and kissed. Then looked at me.

"Monica is your...our gift. We're going to explore tonight, baby," Jen said seductively.

I could tell that Jen had made up her mind about this and seemed beyond excited. And I knew beyond a shadow of a doubt that no matter how good Monica looked or felt or tasted, I would never want to be with anyone but my wife.

"Stop overthinking," Jen continued. "Let's just have some fun."

I said out loud the thought that had been flashing like a neon sign in my mind. "Is this a trick?'

"I think you know that it's not, baby. Let's just enjoy this experience. Okay?"

"You're sure?"

"I'm sure."

Monica stood there smiling at us. "How'd the meeting of the minds go?"

"Just fine. How about we do a shot?" Jen said.

She went over and pulled the tequila and shot glasses out of the kitchen cabinet. Monica opened the fridge and grabbed lime slices.

The three of us stood around the kitchen counter, grinning at each other as we took our shots. I looked at Monica and just started to laugh for some reason. "So you knew about this all along?"

Monica smiled. "Yes, Kent. Jen told me you guys were coming and that you were giving each other experiences for Christmas. She told me about how you meticulously planned this New York trip, just like you... meticulously do *everything*."

"What's that supposed to mean?" I asked, wondering just how much Jen had told her about my...*meticulousness.*

Instead of answering, Jen pulled a baggie out of one of the kitchen drawers and held it up. I saw that it held three edibles. The ones we usually took when we were home alone and in for the night. The ones that made us horny as hell.

"Oh," I said with raised eyebrows.

"Yeah," Jen said with a smile as she pulled out the first edible and placed it in my mouth. She ate the second one and then had Monica open her mouth so she could place the third one on her tongue. Monica grabbed her hand and licked the sugar from her thumb. I felt my jeans tighten again.

Then Jen led Monica over to the couch. Monica was wearing maybe the shortest denim minidress I had ever seen, and the moment she sat down, I could see that she wasn't wearing any panties. In that moment, I decided not to question anything else that night. I would allow my wife to give me this experience and just see where the night took us.

I didn't have to wait long. Monica pulled her dress up, and Jen got on her knees in front of her and put a slice of lime on one thigh and a little line of salt on Monica's other thigh. My dick completely forgot that it was supposed to be behaving and throbbed mercilessly.

"You're doing another shot," Jen said. "Come here."

I walked over to the couch. Jen pulled me down beside her and placed the shot glass perfectly between Monica's legs.

"Lick the salt, take the shot, suck the lime," Jen said with authority.

I looked from her to Monica and back before I fully took in the scene in front of me. I liked the fact that Jen had hair down there, but Monica was almost completely shaved, and I wasn't mad at it. She saw me looking and opened her legs a little wider, showing a glimpse of pinkness. Her clit! It was huge. I was intrigued and not surprised when my mouth started to water.

I reached for the shot.

"No hands!" Jen said, laughing.

I frowned, trying to figure out how to do all three things with no hands.

"Stop thinking!" Monica told me.

I decided to follow her advice. First, I licked the salt from Monica's left thigh and heard her sharp intake of breath. I looked up, and her expression alone almost took me out. I opened my mouth and grabbed the shot, threw my head back, and downed it. I then grabbed the lime with my mouth, my tongue grazing Monica's creamy thigh in the process.

"You're surprisingly good at that," Monica said.

"Oh...you have no idea," Jen said as she stood up. Monica stood up too, and they both positioned me on the couch. Monica unzipped her little minidress and let it drop to the floor, then turned and pulled Jen's top off over her head. She got on her knees and slowly unbuckled Jen's jeans while glancing at me. All I wanted to do was unbuckle my own pants and release my dick, but I didn't know the rules of this new game.

Jen then stepped out of her panties and pulled Monica up to face her. Their two bodies blended beautifully together like a caramel mocha fever dream. I laughed to myself. My edible was definitely kicking in. I just had to get these fucking jeans off.

"You look...uncomfortable. Let us help you," Jen said, reading my expression, as they walked toward me and got to their knees. Monica undid my top button, and then Jen unzipped me. They both grabbed the jeans from around my waist and pulled them down. I didn't have to move an inch as they raised my legs and pulled my pants completely off. Now there was nothing between us except a flimsy pair of boxer shorts.

Not for long, though. The girls turned to each other and started kissing. Monica matched Jen's kissing style perfectly. Jen was an amazing kisser, and I felt my dick somehow harden even more. They noticed it too, turning their attention back to me. Jen leaned in, looking in my eyes as she licked the precum off the tip of my dick. Monica licked her lips, and I felt Jen's hands release me to Monica, who wrapped her hands around my dick, slowly putting the tip in her mouth. It was so wet and warm, I had to look away to gain my composure.

"I don't think he's paying attention to us, Jen..."

I opened my mouth to protest, but Monica picked that moment to deep-throat my dick. She looked at me and slid her mouth down my shaft until I could swear I felt her tonsils. I closed my eyes as I felt Jen's soft hands spreading my legs wider. I took a deep breath and felt myself sink into the couch. Jen joined in, licking at my balls and Monica's tongue all at the same time. Then Jen took my dick out of Monica's hands and sucked me as only she knew how.

"This... this ain't fair," I said laughing. "It's too fucking good."

At that moment, Monica grabbed my dick again, as if they were in competition. *Why was that thought such a fucking turn-on?* Monica moaned like my dick was the best thing she ever tasted. As Jen stroked me, Monica slid me into her mouth, up and down, in and out, slurping like it was the best ice cream cone of her life. Jen stroked me with her left hand while holding Monica's hair up as she sucked me to the point of no return.

"Wait!" I said, too late. I felt myself explode. Monica moaned loudly and sucked harder, then pulled away just in time to watch me spurt right on her cheek and into her hair. I felt compelled to apologize, but Jen licked Monica's face, then my still erupting dick. She took me in her mouth and swallowed the remainder of my cum, something she almost never did. I closed my eyes and allowed the feeling to travel through my legs and down to my toes.

But they weren't done. They pulled me up and both ripped off my shirt as I stood there trying to gain my composure. Then they pushed me toward the bedroom. Once there, I grabbed my wife and pinned her against the wall so I could finally taste those pretty pink lips.

Monica positioned herself on the bed, watching us. I picked Jen up and carried her to the bed. I hovered over her and kissed her lips, her neck, down to her beautiful breasts. Jen rubbed my bald head and closed her eyes. Her breasts were so sensitive. She was the only woman I had ever know who could have an orgasm just from her breasts being sucked.

Monica climbed over and put her mouth on Jen's other breast, while reaching down and touching herself at the same time.

I bit Jen's nipple, causing her to moan even louder. I couldn't wait any more. I reached my hand down between her legs and couldn't believe how wet she was. My dick was officially hard again.

"Damn, baby. You are so wet," I said hoarsely.

"Let me see," Monica said, nudging in beside me. She slid her finger into Jen's pussy, and Jen's eyes widened as she looked at her friend, then me, and back with longing.

"Oooh, shit," Monica said. "You *are* wet. Fuck."

I stood up as Jen slid out from under me and pinned Monica on her back. "Word on the street is that you're *always* wet."

Monica laughed and opened her legs.

"Shit. Look at that, baby," Jen said, looking back at me. "Look how wet we made her."

"What are you gonna do about it?" I asked Jen as I stroked my dick.

I didn't have to say another word. Jen straddled Monica and grinded on top of her, rubbing herself up against Monica's clit. Monica grabbed Jen's hips and moved in sync with her. Their two bodies against each other were taking me there again.

"Fuck," Monica said as Jen climbed off of her and positioned her face between her friend's legs.

This was one sight I never knew I needed to see. Wow. Jen's face was mere inches above Monica's glistening clit.

"So this was what all of your exes were going crazy over, huh?" Jen said to Monica as she leaned in.

Monica's smile faded into a look of ecstasy as Jen took slow little nibbles of Monica's clit. She moved her head up and down as if she was sucking a tiny dick. Which, in essence, she was. Monica's clit was a thing of beauty.

"What does she taste like?" I asked slowly.

Jen raised her head up. "Come see."

I did just that. I took Jen's place on the bed and grabbed Monica's thighs. I buried my face between her legs and finally got to see that clit up close as I pulled it into my mouth, tonguing it like a French kiss. Before I could make another move, I heard Monica's pussy before I saw or felt it. It popped or splashed or maybe exploded was the better word, right in my mouth. Monica let out a scream as she clawed the sheets and then my head, my shoulder...anything she could grab. She came again, even harder, when Jen climbed back in front of me and took another taste of her own.

Monica grabbed Jen's face, grinding slowly, biting her lip. "Oh fuck! Ahhhh, fuck. I'm coming again. Oh shit!"

It was the sexiest thing I'd ever seen. My sweet wife with her innocent face buried in her friend's pussy. Oh shit. I needed to release again. I went and positioned myself behind Jen, looking at Monica's pretty face as I slid into my wife's dripping pussy.

Jen let out a yell and lost her concentration, her mouth hovering over Monica and her eyes closed.

"Oh baby. Yes, yes. Ooooh baby. Oh. My. God!"

Jen was about to come. Hard. I felt her pussy grip my dick, and I lost it seconds before she did, while Monica stared at us and brought herself to yet another orgasm. I opened my eyes to see Monica squirt all over her own hand.

"She's a squirter, baby," Jen said in awe.

"Best Christmas ever," I said as I went in for another taste.

Chapter 3

Not Like Other Girls
by Taina Paso

That was it. She was done with college. Of course, there was still the graduation to attend to and a bunch of other life details. But Felicia had just taken her last final exam and, unsurprisingly, it was something she could've done in her sleep. She was a gifted programmer with a special knack for writing code. And she had finished her program early, completing it in the spring instead of the summer.

"You're like a machine, Fe!" Cecilia had often told her. "You've always got your head in a book. I could see if you actually *needed* to study this much, but this stuff comes so naturally to you."

Cecilia always teased her, saying, "Are you *not* interested in finding a husband? Like the rest of us mere mortals?"

Felicia, in fact, couldn't care less about finding a husband. She didn't even know if she wanted to get married. At 22, she just couldn't understand the appeal. The thought of spending the *rest of her life* with one guy sounded like a nightmare.

What she wanted...what she really longed for was to feel something. Felicia had gone on plenty of dates and was always bored to death. Particularly with people in the same industry as her. Something was missing.

As the oldest kid in her family and with her high level of intelligence, it took a lot to captivate her. Mentally, not many were a match for her wit. She was used to that. What made her feel anything akin to longing was the thought of being dominated. Or taken advantage of. Maybe that wasn't quite right. She wanted her power taken away. She didn't want to have to decide anything. She didn't want to have to *do* anything. That was what appealed to her. And not only did she not want to do anything, she basically wanted to be fucked senseless by more than one man at a time.

The thought of that really got her panties wet. She had abandoned feeling shame about this years ago. But the thing that got in the way was that in this small college town, everyone knew each other—and not only that, but they also knew everything everyone did. Now that she was graduating and would be starting a new life in Seattle soon, Felicia felt like the time was right to fulfill her fantasy. The only problem she had now was figuring out where in the hell to find at least three people to make her dreams come true. She'd been trying to scope out potential mates for over a month now with no luck. Even though she was only looking for a good time, she had to be turned on too. She couldn't just fuck any nitwit. Therein lay her challenge.

It was Friday, and Felicia was feeling pretty good about herself for acing her exams. Any normal 22-year-old might call up her parents or friends to celebrate with them in some sort of way, but all Felicia really wanted to do was get laid. She'd practically been living like a nun for the last three months. That needed to cease tonight.

She decided to go to Smitty's, the local off-campus bar. If nothing else, she could at least gaze upon Brandon. Brandon was the bartender. He might even have even been the owner. He was so fucking hot. Felicia knew for a fact that he wasn't opposed to sleeping with a patron. She had personally witnessed women perched at the bar competing for his attention and him eventually leaving with one. She had only ever admired him from afar. For some reason, Felicia loved studying in bars. Not libraries, but stale, musty, beer-smelling bars. So she had tucked herself away in the corner at Smitty's with her books, never interacting with Brandon. She only knew his name because he was the stuff of legend on campus.

Felicia decided to make a little effort for a change. With her long dark hair, brown eyes, and long, thick lashes, she didn't need much makeup, so a little gloss and mascara went a long way. She had been told that she already dressed like a computer hacker—whatever that was supposed to mean—so when she wore anything other than sweats and a T–shirt, people invariably noticed. She decided to keep it simple, yet sexy. She put on a silky mini slip dress and Doc Martens, pulled her wavy hair out of her customary ponytail, and headed to the bar.

Brandon was behind the bar as usual. Even though it was Friday, things were slow. There were maybe five customers at the most in the entire place. He looked up just as she walked in and did a double-take. But that was all. He was back to wiping and stacking glasses and looking way too busy to give her any thought. Instead of heading to a dark corner, Felicia took a seat at the bar. Eventually, Brandon made his way over to her.

"What can I get you?"

Before she could answer, he yelled over to one of the waitresses to put the CLOSED sign on the door.

"I've gotta warn you, we're closing in a half hour for an event," he told her.

It was at that moment that Felicia realized that she had never actually heard his voice before. Of course, it was deep and raspy. With thick, dark hair that kept falling over his eyes, she fully expected his voice to sound that way. It sent a chill through her entire body.

"Well now, that's a real shame," she said.

"Is it? Why's that?" he asked, looking at her with curiosity.

"Well... first, can I have a shot?"

"Can I have an I.D.?" Brandon said.

Felicia fished her identification out of her purse and handed it over. Brandon held it longer than she expected him to. He looked from her to the I.D. and back again before finally handing it back to her.

"Shot of what?" he asked.

God, he was hot. He had to be at least 6 feet 3 inches of pure muscle. Although Felicia found herself even more attracted to him close up, he was just too sexy to even think about in a relationship way. If she was interested in that, which she wasn't. He was the perfect guy to just fuck, get her rocks off, and start her new, responsible life tomorrow.

"I changed my mind," Felicia told him.

He didn't say anything. He just stood there looking slightly irritated.

"Okay..."

"I'd like to have a Happy Pussy."

"You and probably every other chick in here," he said sarcastically.

"Ha ha. It's vodka, cranberry juice—"

"I know what it is. Coming right up."

With that, he turned around and got busy making her drink. Felicia sat up straight, crossed her legs, and threw her hair over to the other shoulder. Brandon gave her the briefest of glances before he turned his back to her.

She had heard the stories of him sleeping with women from the bar, but he seemed pretty standoffish to her.

She was now convinced that he was the owner. He didn't talk much but did a lot of pointing. Which was hot as hell. He pointed to a waitress, and she nodded, taking off her apron and heading out. He pointed to a busboy and then a table, and that guy also nodded before going to take care of it. A delivery guy walked in, and he pointed over at a table in the corner, where the guy dropped the stuff, tipped his hat to Brandon, and was out the door.

"So it's the Monday of Spring Break," she said. "All the crazy college kids with Daddy's money to spend will be heading this way."

"As much as I hate to miss all of that," Brandon said sarcastically, "I'm closing early for that private party. Here's your drink. Enjoy."

He presented her drink without much fanfare. After the fact, she realized a lot of women probably came into the bar and asked for suggestive-sounding drinks, hoping to get a rise out of him. He didn't seem remotely interested in her, although she had seen him sneaking glances at her while her head was turned.

"I've been in here before," Felicia told him. "You're always so serious. I was hoping to see you crack a smile today."

"I don't smile at people younger than 25. Personal mantra."

"What? How did you..."

Then she remembered he had carded her.

"Why? I was *really* looking forward to that smile. I know for a fact that you *smile* at lots of people, and I don't believe for a second that they're all over 25."

"Believe what you want. But you've got about 10 minutes to finish that drink. In case you haven't noticed, you're the only one here. I'm sure Mom and Dad are getting worried."

"Ooooh, that's not nice," Felicia said facetiously. "I'd be offended if I hadn't been on my own and taking care of Mom, Dad, sister, and brother for years now. I've actually finished my coursework, and I'll be headed to Seattle in three days. To start my very grown-up life."

"Well, good for you," he said with a grin that almost made her feel light-headed. "I'm just kidding with you. I've seen you in here before with your books. All business. I like that. I honestly thought you were older."

"Well, technically I am. It took me five years to finish school because of all the helping of the family thing."

"Hold on," said Brandon as he walked over to lock the door and came back. "Don't want anyone wandering in. But back to you. That's very cool. I always wanted to go to college, but my old man made me an offer I couldn't refuse, and I went from just helping him out to running this place."

"So your dad is Smitty?"

"No. There's no Smitty. He just thought it sounded like a cool name for a bar."

"Hmm, I see. But it's never too late. For school, you know," said Felicia.

"I'm 35. I'll cut my losses. The bar does all right, so I'll just have to survive on my 8th grade education."

Brandon laughed at Felicia's shocked face.

"Kidding. I did make it through high school. Though it was no easy feat."

Felicia was enjoying her Happy Pussy and laughed at herself because she really wanted to take care of her other pussy tonight as well.

"Soooo seeing as I'm leaving town soon and I'm no longer a college student.... I came here...to..."

Brandon leaned in closer to her, looking her in the eyes. "Spit it out, little girl."

"Come on now," Felicia said, uncrossing and recrossing her legs to give Brandon an idea of where she was going with this. "There's nothing *little* about me. I can't tell you how disappointed I am that you're closing early. Here, it took me all these weeks to work up the nerve to talk to you."

"Talk to me? What could you possibly want to talk to me about?"

"Well, you got me there. I don't actually want to *talk* to you."

"Hmmm, interesting. What *do* you wanna do? Keep crossing your legs and flashing the bartender?"

"No. I'd like you to take me in a back room somewhere and fuck my brains out. I've been studying and making sure that I'm in the top five percent of my class," Felicia told him as she finished the last of her drink and leaned forward. "I'm so horny I'm about to lose my mind."

"Take you in the back and fuck you, huh? Wow."

"I know that sounds terrible and not like a nice girl at all. Well, I don't want to be a nice girl tonight. I need to be fucked. Are you sure about that party?"

"Oh, absolutely. The party is happening, but it's only a few of my boys stopping by. I can take you in the back, but they'll be here any minute, and they're gonna get jealous."

"Why? I'd love to fuck them too."

Even as the words left her lips, Felicia didn't know what the hell had gotten into her. Yes, it was her fantasy, but she was in no way prepared to act on it tonight. That is...until she saw the look in Brandon's eyes.

"You serious?"

"Mmm-hmm."

"You wanna fuck me *and* my friends?"

"I do."

"Shiiiiit," Brandon said as he headed over to respond to the pounding on the door.

In walked three guys that were equally as hot as Brandon, if not hotter. How was that possible?

"Are all you guys on steroids? My God!"

"Absolutely not," Brandon said. "We like to work hard in the gym... and everywhere else," He winked at her and started introducing his friends.

"Who is *this*?" the first one said, looking her up and down as he rubbed his hands together.

"This, gentlemen, is Felicia. Felicia has just completed her program over at the college and is looking to let off a little steam. She's hoping we can help her," Brandon said with a mischievous gleam in his eye.

"Felicia, huh? A beautiful name for a fucking smokeshow. Wow. Welcome to Smitty's after dark! I'm Jeremy, that's Will, and the weirdo staring at you is Aaron. So pleased to meet you," the tallest one said eagerly.

"How about some shots?"

"Yes, tequila!" Felicia agreed.

"No more Happy Pussy?" Brandon said.

Brandon's friends exchanged bemused expressions.

"Oh, that's her drink," Brandon explained.

"You don't say," Will said as he pulled up a stool to sit next to her. "How long have you known Brandon?"

"I'm afraid that we won't be getting to know each other in that way tonight, gentlemen. I need that shot and then I need to be fucked. Simple as that."

Brandon and his three friends took a beat and then all broke out into huge grins. While Felicia might have thought she was being spontaneous and risqué, it became obvious that this wasn't the first time the group of friends had done something like this. With their physiques and easygoing personalities, women were always drawn to them.

Brandon poured a round of shots and cranked up the music.

The group toasted to Felicia's accomplishment, and she then wandered over to the dance floor and let the boys see what they would be working with. The slip dress she was wearing showed every curve. The bar was slightly cool, so her nipples were on full display. It was also obvious that she wasn't wearing panties. Felicia noticed Will staring at her. He was about Brandon's height, but Black with dreadlocks. She had never slept with a Black guy before. Guess that ended tonight.

She walked over to him, turned around, and danced suggestively, grazing his jeans with her ass. She raised her hands up over her head, running her fingers through her hair, over her breasts, then slid them down her hips, swaying to the music.

Will wasted no time. He pulled her to him so that she could feel his hardness on her back. She reached behind her, wrapping her arm around the back of his neck while she continued to grind into him, making eye contact with all three men at the bar, who were staring, mesmerized. Both Jeremy and Aaron made their way over to her while Brandon leaned back against the bar, smiling lazily at her. He liked to watch.

As she rolled her body against Will, she grabbed Jeremy around the neck and kissed him, finally starting to feel her body relax. Jeremy ran his hands over her breasts, like he had been waiting a lifetime to do it. Felicia kissed him, reaching down to massage what had caught her eye from across the room. Wow. Brandon's friends were no joke. She couldn't have planned this better if she'd tried.

Jeremy and Will led her over to the bar, where Jeremy bent her over and caressed her ass. In the matter of a minute, she felt his tongue flicking inside of it. He clearly understood tonight's assignment.

"It's just too pretty in that silk for me to resist it," he said.

"Nah, man, look at her titties," Will said. "Those motherfuckers are a work of art. Damn, Brandon, where the fuck did you find her?" He continued to stare at Felicia.

"Yeah, those are some pretty titties," Jeremy agreed.

Felicia was relishing every bit of the attention. She had always been fascinated by the idea of a gangbang but had never truly believed she'd have the opportunity to make it happen.

"Come here," Brandon said, walking over to her. He picked her up and put her on the shiny bar that he had just cleaned. He positioned himself between her legs and kissed her before sliding the straps of her dress off of her shoulders, exposing her breasts. She heard Wil gasp and curse under his breath before he walked over to her.

"I need at least one of those in my mouth. Now," he said as he and Brandon both started to squeeze and knead her breasts.

Felicia knew it was ridiculous—she was perched on the counter of some seedy college bar—but she felt like a goddess.

"What are you waiting for?" she said to Aaron and Jeremy as they stood watching.

With Will on her right and Brandon on the left, Aaron walked behind the bar and stood behind her. Felicia felt his hands grab her thighs from behind, pulling her legs open. Will repositioned himself with his mouth and her breasts, biting her. The sensation went to the tips of her toes and right back to her pussy.

She leaned back into Aaron's hard body, allowing herself to be on full display for the first taker.

Jeremy unbuckled his pants and let them drop, stepping out of them. Felicia could already see the bulge. It was one of the biggest she'd ever seen. She took a deep breath and swallowed and could see Brandon observing her and then deciding to pour everyone another round of shots.

He walked over and held hers up to her lips. She swallowed it down as the group did the same. She leaned back farther into Aaron, and then Jeremy made his move. He grabbed Felicia's hips and pumped into her hard.

Felicia yelped with surprise and a bit of pain until her body was able to adjust to his size. After about a minute or so of the unspeakable pleasure of Jeremy's dick seeming to hit crevices inside of her that she didn't know was there, he pulled out and turned her over onto her stomach. Aaron raised her up like she was a ragdoll, and then she was on all fours. She felt Will's beard graze her ass, which clearly seemed to be his favorite part of her. He kissed and licked it, and Felicia could swear his tongue felt like a tiny dildo the way he worked it in and out. She could feel her pussy getting wetter in response.

She felt Will shift and heard another belt buckle dropping to the floor and then he grabbed her around the waist and slid into her ass.

Felicia was grateful it wasn't Jeremy ripping her ass in two. She could tell Will was smaller but just the right size for what he was doing.

As Will fucked her ass, she looked up and finally saw Brandon taking off his pants. Aaron repositioned her again so her face was directly lined up with Brandon's throbbing manhood. He smiled that lazy smile.

"Open that pretty mouth for me, baby."

She did. Brandon stroked her chin and her hair and then grabbed her head, practically fucking her in the mouth.

She gagged but was so turned on by the feeling of being used this way, she quickly adapted to Brandon's roughness.

Will must've liked what he felt and saw because she felt and heard his loud orgasm as he shot hot cum into her ass. He smacked her ass as he came, and she bit Brandon's dick. Instead of withdrawing in pain, he seemed to like it, and Felicia bit again.

"Oh yeah, shit! Eat that dick. Fuck yeah!" Brandon yelled as he grabbed a fist full of her hair and pumped into her mouth.

Felicia felt new hands around her waist. Aaron. As he turned her body around, Brandon withdrew from her mouth and helped Aaron place her on her back on the bar. Felicia laughed to herself that she had never made it to the backroom with these guys. All the action was on the bar.

"Open your mouth, baby girl," Brandon said as he stood over her face, working his dick with his right hand and squeezing her breast with his right.

Jeremy was back in between her legs, fucking her again. She couldn't believe how wet she continued to be. Jeremy pumped as Brandon worked his hand faster. It was as if they were having a contest. Jeremy won when he pulled out of her and came all over her stomach. Brandon squirted on her face, mouth, and neck, and she looked him in the eyes as she licked it off of her lips. She pulled Brandon to her so that she could suck the remnants straight from the source. Felicia felt the cum running out of her ass, dripping off her stomach, and dripping down her face and neck. She had never felt more spent or more satisfied.

Four men, with their pants down and dicks out and one naked woman sprawled across the bar froze as they heard keys unlock the bar door.

Felicia had a thousand thoughts at once. Was it the police? Had someone complained about the noise? No, the police wouldn't have keys.

No one moved, so she didn't either. A sexy, older version of Brandon sauntered into the bar and looked around, quickly taking in the crazy scene, and then smiled. "You boys couldn't have called me?"

"Fuck Dad, I keep telling you to call first," Brandon said.

Chapter 4

Boss

by Edgar Phipps

Charlie sat back in her chair and breathed a deep sigh of relief. Well, relief and...fear? Was that what she was feeling? Maybe anxiety was a better way to describe it. At 45, she had finally attained her dream position. She was the director of external affairs for a healthcare organization. It was a big deal. For her, anyway. She had been on many teams and had even led some in a project management capacity. But this was different. Five people would be reporting to her, and she was in charge of her own department. They weren't just reporting to her in terms of whatever project she was heading up; this was her actual, full-time team! She could articulate her own vision and really make a difference for the organization. That was the goal, anyway. She was inheriting three staff members, an administrative assistant, a marketing coordinator, and a grant writer. She had to hire a social media person and another grant writer. She had hired the social media manager yesterday, and the person that just left her office was a shoo-in for the grant writer role. In fact, she was too good for this position. For this company, really. She had just relocated to Chicago for her PhD program and had extensive experience in grant writing. Charlie felt lucky to have caught this young woman while she was in a transitional state because that was the only way they could afford to retain someone like her. It was too bad; she could only sign up for a three-month contract to help the department get up and running, and then Alexis had to do a rotation in DC for her program. But Alexis was so impressive that Charlie would've given her a one-day contract to have someone of her caliber lend their expertise to the department. After the three months was up, she'd have to determine if she needed to replace her or if the other grant writer would be enough to support the department. Luckily, Alexis didn't seem at all concerned with the health care center's salary. She had stated that the most important thing to her was helping people and doing work related to her PhD curriculum.

Charlie decided to call Jason with an update.

"What's up, boss lady?"

Charlie got up to close her office door, although she was alone. No one was in the office yet. Her team would be reporting to her for the first time tomorrow.

"Stop it. You're such a hater," she told her best friend.

"You're damn right I'm a hater. You get your own team to mold into whatever you want while I'm stuck over here reporting to Dan's goofy ass."

"I would hire you, but I can't afford you," Charlie laughed.

"Ha ha, you're damn right with those wack social worker salaries y'all posted. So you've hired everybody you need?"

"Oh. My. God. That's why I called you. You remember that girl I told you about, Alexis?"

"Yeah..."

"Well, I just finished her second interview. I offered her the job on the spot. She was even more extraordinary this time. I couldn't chance her getting away from me."

"You mean those big ole boobs getting away from you," Jason said.

"Mannnn, she dresses so conservatively," Charlie said. "You would never know all that was going on. But in addition to the breasts and the hair and the smooth, chocolate skin...is the intelligence. She might be the smartest person I've ever talked to in my life. And she's gonna be reporting to me... I'm not worthy."

"Hmmm. First of all, *I'm* the smartest person you've ever talked to. And you always have the best shit happening to you."

"Look at you! You're so jealous. Stop being a hater, and good things can happen for you too. Besides, I wish she didn't look like she did. I mean, she'll be a brilliant grant writer. I have no doubt about that, but I am keeping it 100 percent professional. I have my own team for the first time, and I am not gonna mess it up lusting after somebody's child."

"Child? I thought you said she was working on a PhD," Jason said. "How old is she?"

"Twenty-five."

"Twenty-five? Well, that's not a *child* child. She's older than your kids..."

"Shit. Not by much. Anyway, say a prayer for me. I don't want her picking up on any kind of vibes from me. This job means too much."

"Send her my way," Jason said slyly.

"Stop it, you old whore. You're the same age as me."

"Yeah, but I'm not her boss."

Charlie really wanted everything to go well with her new job. She realized that she had slept with someone at every place she'd worked. But this was the first time she was in charge. She would be sleeping with no one.

After a couple of weeks, Charlie had to admit that her team was running like a well-oiled machine. Her team of five was working out really well. Somehow, and not on purpose, she had ended up with a team of five women, ranging in age from 24 to 60. The two people she had hired herself were millennials. Charlie felt like she would be able to write a management book after figuring out how to effectively manage millennials, Gen Xers, and baby boomers all on the same team. Alexis specifically was a joy. She was passionate, focused, and hard-working. She was also extremely serious. From what she had shared with Charlie, she came from a strict, religious family and still held true to the beliefs and routines that she had grown up with. Charlie giggled to herself, remembering how she had shared with Jason that Alexis dressed like a Mormon. Which was fine, considering she worked as hard as one too.

"Sooo this Taste of Chicago. What's it all about?" Alexis said one morning after their team meeting ended.

"Well, I haven't been in years. It belongs to the tourists now. But you'd have fun. Are you going?" Charlie asked.

"I do want to go, in spite of your negativity. I was wondering if you'd wanna go with me."

Charlie frowned. First, because there was no way she wanted to go to the Taste and be among throngs of people. Second, because she didn't think it was a good idea.

"I know what you're thinking. You don't think it's a good idea to hang out with your subordinate. Which I guess is why you keep turning down my invitations to lunch," Alexis said as she leaned in the doorway of Charlie's office. "But keep in mind, I'm only here for three months, remember? So pretty soon I won't be your subordinate anymore."

"I may or may not have been thinking exactly that," Charlie told her. Today, Alexis had her dark curly coils in a pouf on top of her head. She was wearing a light summer type of sweater, but it was more low-cut than she had ever seen Alexis wear. Which for Alexis was not really low-cut at all, but Charlie could see and appreciate her cleavage. Alexis seemed completely unaware of the vibe she gave off. To be so young, she was extremely confident. But not in an off-putting way. The way she came into Charlie's office and sometimes perched herself on the corner of Alexis' desk...the way she'd lean in the doorway to share some insights about her work were almost more than Charlie could bear. It turned her on even more that Alexis seemed so innocent and unaware of her appeal.

"Oh wow! Damn," Ahmad said as he entered her office while she was talking to Alexis.

"What's the matter? You're here to fix the printer, right?" Charlie asked him.

He stared at Alexis like he had never seen a woman before.

"Ahmad! Printer...."

"So you're Alexis? You write nice emails. I didn't think you'd look like...this," Ahmad said as he continued staring. "It's like Destiny's Child back here with all of you beautiful women. It's like you're Wonder Woman, and these are your people."

"Ahmad…you're familiar with the Me Too movement, I'm sure. You've gotta work on your professionalism," Charlie half-joked. Ahmad didn't offend her. She thought he was funny, but she had to protect the women on her team, and she never wanted them to feel objectified.

"You are absolutely right, Ms. Charlie. I am a work in progress, but I'm only human."

After Ahmad left, Charlie asked Alexis a question. "Are you even aware of the effect you're having on… some of the staff since you've started?"

It was a loaded question. Charlie was really thinking of herself. Alexis was having an effect on her. Intelligence really was her aphrodisiac. And the pretty smile, soft, luscious body, and wicked sense of humor that Alexis possessed just made things worse.

"Uhhh, effect?" Alexis said modestly. "I don't pay attention anymore to anybody's response to me. All my life, I've been passed over for girls with lighter skin, I guess, so I learned a long time ago to not attach my self-worth to what any guy thinks."

"What about your boyfriend?"

"What about him?" Alexis said. "Well, I guess I should say, I actually don't have a boyfriend. I had one once in high school, and it ended kind of traumatically, sooooo...haven't dated anyone since then."

Charlie leaned forward in her seat as Alexis sat on the edge of her desk.

"You had a boyfriend...once? High school was over ten years ago."

"Yep, that's right. I just don't have an interest. I'm pretty busy, you know," Alexis said.

Charlie thought that explained a lot. With no boyfriend and seemingly no interest in men, it made sense why she was so oblivious to attention.

"So...will you grace me with your presence? To the Taste of Chicago?"

Charlie scrunched up her nose. "It's a NO for me, Dawg. I just can't. Maybe some other time/event."

Alexis smiled mischievously, and Charlie knew there would be another invite at some point.

"I don't know why you wanna hang out with an old woman like me anyway. I'm sure you have way cooler people your age. I'm literally picking up my grandson when I leave here," Charlie told her.

Alexis stood straight up and backed away from Charlie's desk. "Whose grandson?"

"My grandson."

"You mean by marriage or something, right?"

Charlie laughed. "No, I mean by way of my son making me a grandmother when he was 17, making me a grandmother at 40. And now Joshua is seven."

Alexis shook her head in disbelief.

"Okay! Several things. First, you're old enough to have a 24-year-old? Secondly, you have grandchildren?! Third, you're *47!?*

"Yes, your math skills are impressive," Charlie laughed. "You are doing amazing things for my ego right now."

"Woman, you are beautiful. I mean, that much was already obvious. But I figured you for this childless boss lady who screamed at kids to get off her condo lawn."

"Not sure if condos have lawns, but yeah... I hear that a lot. Nope. I'm an old woman."

Alexis grinned at her. "Even when you're actually an old woman...you will never be an old woman. Wow, you just became even more fascinating to me. I'm officially intrigued. And for the record, I think you are so cool. I would be honored to hang out with you any time. Over any person *my age.*"

Over the course of the next few weeks, Charlie's team continued to be amazing. Things were going smoothly, and she had started to relax a bit more into her role.

Alexis' time with her would be drawing to a close soon, and in spite of herself, she had really grown fond of her grant writer and was beginning to think of her as a friend. Although with a 23-year age gap, they had absolutely nothing in common. Charlie continued to be surprised that Alexis wasn't turned off by her lifestyle. She didn't really consider herself a practicing bisexual, but she had been with several women. They always seemed to seek her out, and she didn't mind it. She was physically attracted to women but had never met one that she thought about in more than a physical way. Until now. She thought about Alexis a lot. Much more than she was comfortable with. But there was nowhere to go with those thoughts. Alexis was too young, pretty much a virgin, and not gay. In fact, she had shared with Charlie that she followed the Bible pretty closely and thought homosexuality was a sin. Although she judged no one. She believed everyone was on their own journey to find God in their own way. Charlie had no interest in hooking up with a 20-something religious virgin. That definitely did not sound like a good time. So she hid her attraction to Alexis and did her best to create a great working environment for her team. All of them.

One Saturday morning, Charlie was heading to a board meeting. She had joined a board a few months ago and was still getting the hang of it. It was a lot of responsibility, heaped on top of all her other responsibilities. She hadn't slept well, tossing and turning, trying to think of innovative ways to be impactful both on the board and with her job.

She was surprised to see a text come through from Alexis. *On a Saturday?* she thought. *Hmmm.*

I'm in the crowd at the Taste and I thought I smelled your perfume. Are you here?

Charlie stared at her phone. Who would send their boss a text like this? On a Saturday, no less. What was up with this girl? Did she know how she sounded?

She responded to Alexis that she was on her way to a board meeting and couldn't wait to get back home because she was sleep deprived.

You're still having trouble sleeping? You poor thing. You should come sleep in my bed.

Charlie stared at her phone yet again. This girl was not gay, not bi. Not anything. But damn if she didn't sound like she was *flirting*. She laughed to herself and texted Alexis back.

You know…if I didn't know better. I swear, sometimes it seems like you're flirting.

Charlie regretted the words the instant she pressed SEND. She wanted no awkwardness in the office. Even though Alexis would be leaving soon, she didn't want to offend her. Another text from Alexis came through.

And what if I was…

Charlie was attempting to keep her eyes on the road, but *this* text… What? She wondered what exactly Alexis was thinking. She had experienced women in the past who knew of her orientation and flirted with her not because they were interested, but because they thought that since she was attracted to women, she must be attracted to all of them. Not so. At any rate, she didn't know what had gotten into Alexis, but she had no interest in going down that rabbit hole.

Come over tonight. I'll make you dinner and let you get a good night's sleep. In my bed.

Charlie was frozen. She drove for a bit but didn't want to be rude and possibly hurt Alexis' feelings, so she just sent a laughing emoji and prayer hands, to say, *Ha Ha and thanks for thinking of me.* She then told Alexis that she was pulling up to her building and she'd talk to her later. She turned off her phone and went to her meeting.

The next Monday at work, the day was uneventful. Alexis was polite as always and didn't give any indication that her feelings were hurt.

At the end of the day, however, Alexis was the last one to leave for the evening. Charlie, working late once again, sat frowning at her computer screen.

"Long day?" Alexis asked as she poked her head into the office.

"Oh my God. I still can't sleep, and I need to finish this report before I go. My eyes are starting to cross," Charlie said as she stretched and massaged her aching neck.

"Here... let me," Alexis said, as she walked over to Charlie's desk and stood behind her chair. The next thing Charlie knew, Alexis was kneading her shoulders...then her neck. Charlie froze as she felt Alexis' fingers slide into her hair, massaging her scalp. It felt so good. Charlie kept opening her mouth to tell Alexis, 'No thank you, I'm fine.' But the words never came. What did come was an involuntary wetness between her legs. Fuck.

"Ummm, Alexis..."

"Shhhhh, you work so hard. I have really loved working with you. I hate that I have to leave in a week. I'm gonna miss you."

With that, Charlie felt the undeniable touch of soft lips on her neck. She continued to sit frozen at her desk. In disbelief. This was not good.

"Let me cook dinner for you tonight. I have been begging you to hang out with me. I've never had to work this hard for a friendship in my life," Alexis said with a hint of sadness in her voice.

It was true. Charlie had turned down every invitation that Alexis had extended to her. She had been in a funk. She'd been single since her divorce years ago. All she did was go to work and the gym...maybe a nice getaway every once in a while, but she had not connected with another person—a real connection— in a very long time. She was just about to refuse yet again, when Alexis suddenly spun her chair around, and Charlie was eye to chest with Alexis' beautiful double Ds.

And then Alexis bent down and kissed her.

Soft and sweet, gently on her lips. "I'm not taking no for an answer. Unlock your phone."

"What?" Charlie said breathlessly, while she did as she was told.

"That's my address. I'll see you at 7," Alexis said and then waltzed out of her office.

As Charlie drove home later, she had 100 percent decided she was going to send Alexis a text and respectfully decline. When she got to a stop light and picked up her phone, a text from Alexis popped through.

Don't even think of trying to stand me up. I've already started the lasagna, and I have your Santa Margherita chilling...

Charlie sat at the light, dumbfounded, staring at her phone until the car behind her honked. She made her way home, still trying to figure out a way to get out of this dinner date.

By the time she made it home, she'd had a change of heart. Alexis was a sweet girl. A wonderful person. She was a wonderful person. Two wonderful people would have a wonderful night...no matter what happened. Right?

Two hours later, she found herself sitting at Alexis' little dining room table, finishing her second glass of pinot. Dinner had been great, and she was enjoying herself. Alexis had been torturing her all night, walking around in boy shorts and a bra top. She felt like such a creep, lusting after this beautiful young woman, who somehow, for some reason, seemed enamored by her.

"You know...I was already gonna give you a glowing reference for your next job. You didn't have to cook for me," Charlie said, laughing.

Alexis took the glass from Charlie's hand gently and led her over to the area of the studio where her bed was.

Charlie frowned up at Alexis as she pushed her back to a seated position on the bed. What was this girl, who had only had sex once, gonna do for her? Before she could have another thought, Alexis had sandwiched herself between Charlie's legs. She bent down and graced Charlie with another soft kiss. This one lasted longer, and Charlie felt that familiar wetness once again. She had worn a short little sundress, and Alexis placed her knee up against Charlie in a way that made her gasp.

She pushed Charlie onto her back and straddled her.

"What are you doing?" Charlie said incredulously. Alexis had been making her feelings known, but Charlie had not taken her seriously at all. "You're not gay or bi or…even interested in intimacy. That's what you said!"

"That's until I met you," Alexis said with a raspy voice as she continued to trail kisses from Charlie's lips to her neck and then chest.

Charlie was dizzy with lust. She was so wet. Had she given off sexual vibes to Alexis without realizing it? Where was this coming from?

"Look. I know you think this is out of the blue. I know you think I'm young and experienced, and you probably don't wanna waste your time," Alexis said shyly. "Everybody at work wants you. They come to me, asking if you're single and I swear I get jealous. I'm not bisexual. I'm not attracted to women. I'm attracted to *you.* You're amazingly beautiful. And brilliant and so funny. And driven... and hot! I don't know what else to say. But I've never wanted anything as bad as I want you."

With that, Alexis slid Charlie's straps down her shoulders and pulled off her little sundress. She lay on the bed watching Alexis take off her own clothes and decided she would stop resisting. She was about to get up and take the lead, like she always did with women, but Alexis pushed her back, shaking her head.

"Uh-uh. You're always in charge. Always running the show, making sure everyone else is okay. Let me just try...to take care of you."

Alexis continued trailing kisses down her neck, and Charlie closed her eyes and relaxed. She was helpless anyway. She hadn't been touched by anyone in years. It felt so good to just allow herself to be made love to.

Alexis's warm mouth was on Charlie's breast, and she felt lightheaded. Alexis caressed and sucked ever so gently as she took her other hand and slid Charlie's damp panties off.

"Oh." Alexis' eyes widened when she saw how wet Charlie was. "I did that?" she asked with what appeared to be pride. Her eyes were half-mast, and she licked her lips before positioning herself between Charlies' legs.

"Mmmm, you smell amazing," Alexis said as she kissed Charlie's thigh softly. She kissed her other thigh and all around the parts that Charlie was usually impatient for people to get to. But this night was different. It was the first time in her life that she didn't feel like she had to *do* anything. Alexis wanted nothing from her. Charlie realized in that moment that sex had been performative for her. She liked being the aggressor and blowing people's minds. But this beautiful young woman wanted nothing more than to make sweet love to her, and it felt incredible.

She felt Alexis' small hands on either side of her thighs and then her mouth. Oh God, her mouth! She alternated between gentle kisses and little nibbles, and Charlie could not believe how good it felt. Maybe because it had been so long and maybe because she actually really liked Alexis. She heard herself moaning before she was even aware that the sounds were coming from her.

The more she moaned, the more turned on Alexis seemed to be. This was a new, aggressive side of her. She grabbed Charlie's ass and buried her face in between her legs, and Charlie released. She was momentarily scared that all the ensuing wetness would be off-putting for Alexis, but no. Alexis slurped and moaned, and when Charlie glanced down at her, she looked like she was in a trance, under a spell. Charlie couldn't help but feel a little burst of pride that this woman, who could really have anybody she wanted, man or woman, wanted *her*. And she let Charlie know just how badly over and over again for the rest of the night.

Charlie couldn't wait to call Jason.

Chapter 5

New Traditions

by Kali Parks

I sat on the couch looking at the calendar app on my phone. Friday was my 11th wedding anniversary. I had been married to Jimmy for over a decade. It was a good marriage, and I was happy. Maybe content was a better word. Jimmy was a wonderful man and a great husband, but I knew him better than he knew himself. I had always read that the dynamic in a marriage changes once you know everything there is to know about a person. I tried to think of what Jimmy could do to excite me or catch me off guard, and I came up blank. I didn't have an interest in anyone else, and divorce would never cross my mind. But there was a sense of longing I had been feeling for a while. Maybe I'd dye my hair...or better yet, invest in some sexy lingerie to spice things up. I had lingerie that I had bought when we first got married, but Jimmy had practically laughed me out of the bedroom when I tried to use furry handcuffs, cuff him to the bed, and dance seductively for him. He had smiled politely and said, "Good job, baby. That was nice. Want some ice cream?" The way one would after having watched their kid in a recital.

We still enjoyed our sex life and had a good time but had come to the conclusion that kink and lingerie just wasn't for us. I still managed to get him to loosen up with a pretty regular end-of-the-week blow job, but even that was becoming a bit routine. The last time he had just thanked me, like I'd made his favorite meal or something. Jimmy and I were so busy with our careers, sex had become an afterthought. Maybe that was the problem. Jimmy was an accountant, and I was a systems analyst. We had both spent our entire careers and earned great money being analytical, detail-oriented, and living in our heads. I loved that we had that in common, but it didn't seem to translate well to the bedroom.

I was bored. I had to admit it to myself before I could do anything about it. What to do, though? With our anniversary quickly approaching, I needed to figure it out.

"Planning world domination over there?" Jimmy said from across the room.

"Actually, I was just thinking about our anniversary. The big eleven," I said. "What do you wanna do?"

"Eleven years huh?" Jimmy said, rubbing his beard, which had a lot more gray in it these days. "What does one do for year eleven?"

"We could go to—"

"Bavette's? Or STK? Sure, you want me to make the reservation?" Jimmy said, further making me feel like Predictable Patty.

"No. Not Bavette's or STK or any other restaurant downtown," I said. "Let's do something...different."

Jimmy stood up and stretched. His faded pajama pants were older than our relationship. "Whatever you come up with, honey. I'm sure it'll be fine," he said as he walked over and kissed me on the forehead. "I gotta go drop the kids off at the pool."

I closed my eyes and winced as my husband walked away. "You've gotta stop saying that. Please just go to the bathroom without the announcement."

Jimmy just gave a thumbs up without turning around. Even though there was only ever one person in the room, he was notoriously bad at reading it. I absolutely despised the various ways he announced to me that he was on his way to do number two.

I sighed heavily. No, we weren't going downtown for yet another anniversary dinner. I had to come up with something else.

"Why don't you have a threesome?" Brenda said the next day at work. "You know he's not leaving you, and you're not going anywhere. You guys are solid. So get a little plaything."

I looked at her like she had grown a third eye. "I'm attempting to spice things up... not *blow* them up. Besides, I... *we* barely have enough energy for each other. You want me to add another person to the mix? Come on now.?

Brenda smiled as she bit into her sandwich. "I'm just kidding. Honestly, I'm only on year five, but the thing that keeps Bill and me excited is travel. New, exotic places, you know?"

Of course, I had thought about taking a trip. Somewhere we had never been. But it was so hard for both of us to get away from work at the same time. One of us was always in the middle of a project, and it took months of strategic planning for either of us to feel comfortable taking time off.

I was concerned about more than just our anniversary coming up. I just wanted to feel general excitement about my husband. The way I used to. I didn't feel like things were getting to the point where we needed counseling or anything. But I definitely wanted to shift our paradigm in some way.

I decided that in order to have a more exciting marriage, I needed to be a more exciting person. Woman. A more exciting woman. Starting today.

I decided to leave work early and prepare a special meal for dinner. Maybe seafood. I made a detour and picked up the ingredients for a seafood boil. I couldn't remember the last time I'd done that at home. Jimmy and I both loved seafood. I needed to do this more often.

When I made it home and got to the front door, I could hear the TV. I guess I wasn't the only one who had decided to ditch work early.

I burst through the door, bags in hand, and saw Jimmy sitting on the couch, staring at the TV.

"Hey, can you help me with the—"

Our giant living room TV had an equally gigantic man on it. Well, two men. And a woman. One man was holding a small woman down, while the second man was having anal sex with her. Well, anal sex was a nice way to put it. This woman was basically being violated. Or pretending to be.

"Oh!" Jimmy said when he saw me and fumbled to turn the TV off. I had so many questions.

"What is this?"

"Nothing," Jimmy said quickly. "I mean, I just down-loaded this app on my phone on a whim, and it asked if I wanted to login from the TV, and I just did it."

"No! Don't turn it off," I said, turning my head side-ways as I watched a huge penis seemingly tear the tiny woman in half. I frowned and turned to my husband. "You *like* this? Wait! You were watching porn on your phone? For how long? What are you even doing home? Why didn't you tell me you were into porn now?"

Jimmy rushed over to me. "Baby, I'm so sorry. I'm not *into porn* now. I was just bored, and this ad popped up on my phone. I wasn't thinking. I was gonna delete it.

"Delete it. Didn't you just download it?" I asked him.

"Yeah. No. I mean, yeah, I did, but I just wanted to see what the porn of today is like..."

"So you were just doing a comparison of porn quality from past to present," I said sarcastically.

Jimmy looked beyond embarrassed. "You know this isn't me. I really was just bored."

He reached for the remote to turn the TV off once again, and I grabbed his arm. "I'm not mad," I told him and then took his hand and gently pulled him over to the couch. "Sit down. I'm intrigued."

Jimmy followed me to the couch and sat down like a robot. I could feel his eyes burning a hole into the side of my face, but I really wasn't upset with him. We had more in common than I sometimes gave us credit for. If I was feeling a little bored or unfulfilled, then of course he was too.

"Hey," I said, turning to him, "remember that old library I used to work at when I was in school?"

"Yeah," Jimmy said cautiously.

"Can you meet me there tomorrow?"

"Why? You can just serve the divorce papers here."

I burst out laughing. "Stop. There will be no divorce, *but* I do have something I'd like to serve you. The library, 2nd floor, over by the periodicals."

"You mean, where I used to meet you after class, back in the day? How do know it's still secluded?"

"Because one of us still has her library card," I told him. "Now I've gotta make dinner for my freak of a husband. I'll leave you to this. And I promise you... I'm *not* mad."

Not only was I not mad, but I actually felt invigorated. I wasn't the only one who was bored! I thought it might hurt my feelings to know that my husband was watching porn behind my back, and maybe he was bored too, but instead of feeling insecure about it, I felt strangely powerful. The weird, stiff way Jimmy was sitting in front of the TV, mesmerized by what was on the screen told me that it wasn't something he had been doing for a while. He looked like a kid with a new toy who wasn't sure how to work it. He looked innocent to me. And I wanted to be with one to blow his mind. Not his porn app.

The next day, I called off work and went to visit Lizzie's Lace. I hadn't been there in years. Well, since the fuzzy handcuff debacle. But I knew exactly what I was looking for, and this time, my husband would not be politely patting me on the head.

I bought my outfit, went back home (relieved that Jimmy had not beaten me there again), and took my time, making myself look irresistible. I curled my hair, applied makeup, and slipped into my short, pleated skirt, cardigan letterman's sweater, glasses, and two ponytails. From a distance, I could pass for a high school student. Maybe one who had failed a few times, I thought, smiling to myself.

I had to admit I was nervous. Jimmy and I had not done anything outside our norm in a long, long time. But whatever happened, I'd see it through. I wanted my husband to stare at me the way he had been staring at that TV.

I made it to the library about twenty minutes before Jimmy was due to meet me and chatted up old Mrs. Levant. She had been the head librarian for as long as I could remember, and I knew that she was half blind.

There was a blind spot of sorts over in the periodical section, and I happily confirmed that not only was it still there, but it was even more obscured by new shelves that had been added to the area.

I took my coat off, threw it over a chair, and observed the activity down on the first level. I saw my husband walk in, right on time, looking like a nervous schoolboy himself. He glanced up just as I was about to try and get his attention. He did a double-take looking up at me and smiled. This would be fun.

"Hi," I said as he made his way over to me.

"What are you up to? What are you wearing? Wow, you look..."

"What?"

"So fucking hot!"

I walked deeper into our little corner and showed Jimmy that I wasn't wearing anything under my skirt. I was pleasantly surprised when I noticed his eyes get bigger than I had ever seen them. And then he looked around the library frantically, finally settling down when he saw how deserted the place really was.

I positioned him against a wall draped in shadows, turned my back to him, and lifted my skirt.

"What are you doing?"

"I want you to...fuck me in the ass," I told him in no uncertain terms.

Jimmy almost choked on air, his eyes going even wider. "I'm sorry, what? You don't like that."

"I don't *not* like it. But I wanna try it. The video...the porn the other night was hot. So, baby, please take it. Like in the video."

"Baby," Jimmy said, but all the while, I saw the bulge beginning to build in his pants. "I don't want to hurt you."

"You've heard the phrase *hurt so good*, right? So stop talking and give me what I need."

I turned my back to him again and lifted up my skirt. I heard his intake of breath and then his zipper. He held my hip with his left hand and gently tried to enter me.

"Oh, wait!" I said, as I pulled lube out of my pocket. "Use this."

"Who are you?" Jimmy said as he took the lube from me and shyly placed it at the opening.

"I think we'll need more than that," I said to him over my shoulder.

Jimmy squirted out a nice, liberal amount and proceeded to ease into me. Initially, the pain was instant, and I saw stars. But I bit my lip and moaned quietly to egg him on. Jimmy sucked in his breath and grabbed my waist tighter as he succeeded in getting the tip in. I felt myself contract and push him out voluntarily. I grabbed the rail in front of me and bit my lip.

"Want me to stop?"

"No! I think I might like this. Put it in again. Please."

"Shit...when you beg like that."

This time, Jimmy was a bit more aggressive and slid into me. I could hear his breathing and feel his hands gripping my hips.

"Damn, baby. Damn!"

Just as I was beginning to think that not only could I get used to this, but I might actually like it because it was a completely different sensation, Jimmy grabbed me and forgot all about being gentle. He was breathing so hard I almost had to shush him. Ms. Levant might've been blind, but she wasn't deaf, and we were just about the only two people in the whole place. I felt Jimmy shoot hot and fast into me with a guttural grown that turned me on even more. "Oh wow. Shit," he groaned, depleted.

He slowly pulled out and turned me around to face him. "Damn again! That was incredible. What...where did that come from?"

"I thought it was time for a new Friday routine."

Chapter 6

Mistress

by Genevra Lily

Ariel beamed with pride as she pulled away from Mistress Silk's condo. With two degrees under her belt and a wonderful and supportive family, no one would believe what she did for work. Most people believed that you had to be damaged in some way to engage in what was technically classified as 'sex work,' but Ariel was not damaged goods. Like many people, she had stumbled across something that she seemed to have a knack for, and she was now capitalizing on that. In her opinion, there were a lot worse ways to earn the type of money she did. She felt like she was built for this. She always liked to joke with her colleagues that she had not chosen this career. It had definitely chosen her. Since about the age of 12, she had been a taller girl. That had turned into her being a statuesque woman.

Some guys had called her an Amazon or asked if she played for the WNBA. But as she reached her 30s, and curves replaced her long, stick-person-like limbs, she had become what her ex-boyfriend liked to refer to as a *showstopper*. And this career probably wasn't forever. Ariel would do this until she didn't want to anymore.

Everywhere she went, people did a double-take. They didn't know whether to stare at her 5'11 height or her looks. Ariel could acknowledge that people found her stunning, but she would always be humble because the traits that were considered attractive or intriguing about her were the very same things that she had been bullied mercilessly for. Long legs, being taller than the teacher, fair, porcelain skin, red hair, and big gray eyes. She was even bullied for having a mole right above her top lip. It wasn't until she was in high school that someone referred to it as a beauty mark. All that had been *wrong* with her as a teen had become irresistible to men and women alike now that she was an adult.

She pulled into her parking space in back of her condo and opened the folder that was on the passenger seat.

Her first solo assignment!

Ariel laughed to herself, thinking how she had to sign formal documents to accept this assignment. In addition to the standard NDA that some higher profile clients required, this guy also had a check-in form. And Mistress Silk had informed her that this client had paid extra for her specifically.

First, Ariel reviewed his checklist again. This guy wanted to be slapped, punched, kicked, called names, and all manner of things. And he also had a pretty serious foot fetish. Oh, and he wanted to be called Senator. Ariel looked at the next page of the document. He actually *was* a senator. A junior state senator.

Oh, this was going to be fun.

Once Ariel was inside her condo, she went to her closet and pulled out the newest outfit that Mistress Silk had selected for her. She had worn various outfits while working alongside Mistress Silk when she was in training, but never anything like this. The senator had indicated that he really got off on innocent-looking but seemingly serious businesswomen who had a dark side. So Ariel would be wearing what looked, at first glance, like a black business suit. But the blouse was satin and leather, the skirt latex, and the shoes about six inches high. She knew the young senator was six feet tall, so she would tower over him.

When she allowed him to stand, that is.

Ariel had three hours to prepare before she met the senator at the dungeon. After six weeks of serving as a sub and then four more weeks serving with Mistress Silk as a domme, she had developed a very good intuition about what drew high-powered people into this lifestyle. They basically wanted their power taken away. And she was just the girl for the job.

Three hours later, Ariel was sitting in the safe room, waiting for her client. The senator walked in, and Ariel was pleasantly surprised by how attractive he was. It didn't matter in terms of how well she did her job, but when she could look at a client and get turned on a little herself, that was an added plus.

The senator was tall, with sandy blond hair and a boyish charm about him. He was lean, and you could tell that he worked out and took great care of his appearance. But not in an overly metrosexual kind of way. Ariel wondered just how dirty he wanted to get. She went over the previous information with him. Double-checked that he understood the terms, safe words, and how their session would flow. She noticed him stealing shy glances at her, no doubt surprised and maybe even thrown off to see Ariel in her street clothes. But Ariel liked to have the initial check-in without all her gear on to get the sense of a person before the action began. Once all formalities were squared away, Ariel excused herself to go change while the assistant escorted the senator to the dungeon.

Ariel quickly applied her makeup and slid herself into her sexy attire. She stepped into the dungeon to see the senator casually sitting in the corner as instructed.

He looked way too comfortable, and she felt her alter ego beginning to kick in.

"You're here because you deserve to be punished. Stand up."

The senator did as he was told.

"Strip. And then I'm going to collar you. You don't deserve freedom."

The senator hesitated.

"Did I tell you that you could look at me? I said to remove your fucking clothes. See if you can get that right. Do you think you deserve another chance to show me that you can follow instructions?" Ariel said as she walked over and removed her whip from the wall. She gave it a satisfying crack, seeing with satisfaction that she had the senator's full attention.

He rapidly started to remove his clothes, practically buzzing with excitement. Ariel walked around him in slow circles, observing him as he undressed.

Once he was naked, Ariel stood face to face with him. "Assume the position." She motioned for him to bow his head. Then she fastened the leather collar around his neck and led him over to the couch by his leash. Ariel pushed his head down, where he only had a view of her feet. Even though she was wearing heels that did not show her toes, the senator kept stealing glances at her feet. She knew what he wanted, and she was determined to make him work for it.

"Senator?" Ariel said sharply.

"Yes...Mistress."

"Did I tell you that you could look at me?"

"N-No, Mistress," he said timidly.

"Did I tell you that it was okay for you to think about what you'd like me to do to you?"

"No, Mistress."

"On your knees!"

The senator scrambled down to his knees like a little kid preparing for his favorite snack. Ariel couldn't believe he was so timid. She knew for a fact that this particular politician was very much an alpha male in his daily communication. She had watched numerous videos of him giving speeches, leading meetings, and at meet and greets. He was a man that was very sure of himself. But not at that moment. Ariel was beginning to enjoy herself. This was her favorite type of client.

"That's right. I'm going to let you know when you can speak, Senator. Now lick that boot that you're staring at. And if you lick it correctly, I may take it off and let you *look* at my foot. You'd like that, wouldn't you?"

The senator nodded vigorously, still staring down.

"Senator, you may speak. Would you like to look at my foot?"

"Yes, Mistress."

Ariel switched from her whip to a paddle. "On your knees. Yes, Mistress, what?"

"Y- Yes, Mistress, I-I would like to look at your foot. Very much."

"I don't know if I'm convinced," Ariel said seductively. She walked around until she was standing behind him. "Get on all fours."

The senator did as he was told, and Ariel paddled him once. Not too hard, but enough to get his attention. He let out a surprised yelp.

"Senator, why are you on your knees in front of me begging to be whipped like the impotent pussy you are?"

Whack!

Ariel paddled him a bit harder and observed his sharp intake of breath.

"Oh, you like having your ass beat? You're enjoying this?" Ariel said as she continued to circle him.

Whack!

Ariel paddled him even harder and saw him flinch. That's what she was looking for. Then she noticed something else.

"Why is your dick hard? Did I say you were allowed to get hard?"

The senator looked confused, no doubt wondering what the correct answer was and whether or not he should answer.

"I know it's hard for you to figure out what to do. You don't have any constituents in this room. No one cares about how much money you have or how much power. You answer to me in *this* room. Do you understand?"

The senator started to whimper. He really seemed to respond to Ariel's words.

"When I ask you a question, you answer it." Ariel squatted right in front of the senator so that they were face to face, although the senator continued to look at the floor.

"Look at me."

The senator blinked up at her as his brown eyes focused on hers.

"Did I say that you were allowed to get hard? You think that I'm here to get you off?"

"No, Mistress."

Slap!

Ariel slapped the senator across the face.

"Let's try this again." Ariel propped her six-inch stiletto up on the couch. "You can lick it now. See if you can control yourself. I don't want you coming all over my pretty shoes. You understand me?"

"Yes Mistress," the senator said miserably and immediately began tentatively licking at the toe of her shoe.

"That's better, Senator." After Ariel allowed him a few licks, she snatched her foot away from him.

"What did I tell you about that dick? You little bitch. Look at you. You can't even control yourself. What the fuck are you gonna do for me? You don't want to disappoint me, do you?"

Ariel grabbed the senator's leash and led him, like a dog, over to another part of the dungeon. She had the senator sit in a chair, and she stood in front of him. She reached over to her special table and grabbed the nipple clamps. Although the senator was doing a good job of speaking only when spoken to, Ariel decided to take things a step further. She could see his eyes questioning whether this was going to be pleasurable or painful. Ariel wanted to train him to not expect to like the things she was doing to him. They both knew he was there because, in the end, the abuse turned him on. But there was a delicate balance. If he expected to enjoy every aspect of his experience with the Mistress, then there would be nothing for him to work toward.

So Ariel clipped one nipple clamp onto the base of his nipple, and he winced, jumping with a small yelp of pain.

"Yes, that's right. I'm not here for your enjoyment. You are nothing but a sniveling weasel," Ariel said, bending down to eye level with the senator. "You haven't earned the right to feel pleasure. Do you deserve to feel good and sit in front of me with a hard dick?"

"No..."

"No, what?"

"No, Mistress. I don't deserve to—"

"Shut up. I'm tired of hearing your bitch-ass voice," Ariel said as she stood up.

She took the second nipple clamp and placed it on him, squeezing it even tighter as she did so. Ariel watched as he gritted his teeth, trying not to wince in pain.

"Oh, so you can take it, huh? You think you're a real man and you can handle the Mistress's punishment? Hmmm," Ariel said facetiously as she slapped the senator again.

The senator was sitting in his chair, trembling slightly, with his legs pressed together, no doubt to help him endure the pain of the nipple clamps.

Ariel positioned herself between his legs. She used her knee to spread his legs wider apart.

"Look at me," she told him.

The senator looked up at Ariel expectantly. She placed her heel between his legs. She enjoyed the way his eyes moved rapidly from her body to his nipple clamps to her foot, trying to figure out what she would do next.

Ariel could tell from his reactions that he had never been with a dominatrix before. Even though Mistress Silk had shared with her that he was a novice, she hadn't really believed a man this successful had never decided to indulge in this type of play before.

He was so eager to indulge that it turned Ariel on a bit. She decided to turn his eagerness into something else. She took a stiletto heel and positioned it right above the senator's balls. She observed an interesting mix of fear, trepidation, and excitement happening all at once with him. She placed her heel onto his scrotum sack and heard his gasp. She slowly increased her pressure until she heard his unmistakable whimpering.

"Shut the fuck up. You deserve this! Why the fuck can't you do what you're supposed to do? Look at you," Ariel said as the senator's nose began to run. He was almost at the limit of what he could stand. She removed one of the clamps from the base of his nipples and placed it right onto the tip. He bit his lip and squirmed, trying not to make noise.

"Oh no you don't. Shut the fuck up. Did I tell you that you could make a sound?"

"No, Mistress!"

With that infraction, Ariel repositioned the other nipple clamp as she increased the pressure between the senator's legs. She watched the beads of perspiration form on his forehead as he whimpered in pain. She dug her heel in a little harder, and the senator pursed his lips, grabbing his chair with both hands to keep from screaming out.

Ariel then took the senator's hands and secured them over his head onto the wall behind him. Now he was really helpless.

"I know what you want. Mistress always knows what you want," she told him.

She removed her stiletto and placed her foot on the senator's shoulder as he turned slightly to try and look at it.

"Don't you fucking move, you piece of shit. When I feel like letting you look at my arch, you'll know."

Ariel took her bare foot and pressed it into the senator's nut sack. He immediately started to moan with his dick becoming harder than ever. Ariel increased her pressure to the point that it should've been painful, but the senator was so turned on by her foot that he dripped a little on her heel.

"You fucking miscreant. You got cum on my foot. What the fuck are you thinking? I tell you when you can come!"

Ariel withdrew her foot and picked up the senator's leash. She pulled it tighter, choking him.

"You'd better not say one word," she told him as he began to turn red. She looked down at the dampness on her foot. "You're gonna clean that up, bitch."

Ariel loosened the leash as the senator gasped for air. She placed her foot on his forehead so that her heel was directly in front of his mouth. "Get rid of that," she said of the drop of precum on her big toe.

The senator was practically shaking with excitement or desire; Ariel couldn't tell. But his pink tongue poked tentatively in and out as he glanced at her briefly before closing his eyes, gagging to try and obey her command. Licking his own cum didn't seem to be something he was accustomed to, but Ariel also noticed that his dick practically throbbed when he did it.

"You call that clean? You get your jizz on me and think you won't have to make it right? Open your fucking eyes and watch what you're doing. If you don't like eating it, then don't let your little adolescent dick drip on me."

The senator whimpered as Ariel took her foot and rubbed it all over his face before returning it to her shoe. She allowed a little slack in his leash and removed his hands from the overhead restraint. She did a quick assessment of his state of mind. He was sweating. He looked a little rattled, maybe nervous about what he had just experienced, but none the worse for wear. They had spent about an hour together, and he had done well for the first visit. She would have to spend time training him on how to respond to her in a way that satisfied her. And the next time, she might even let him look at her toe.

Chapter 7

Cigar Smoke

by Chelsea Wallace

Melissa signed the document with a flourish. No one was ever happy to get a divorce, but she was so relieved to be free of Walter's cheating ass she actually felt like celebrating.

"Are you smiling or crying?" her best friend Ava asked her.

Just hearing Ava acknowledge Melissa's ambivalence made her emotional. She hated that about herself sometimes. She could be strong...until someone called attention to her feelings. Then she would lose it.

"Ohhhhh, no. Oh, babe, it's okay," Ava said, rushing to Melissa's side as unexpected tears streamed down her face.

"I…I don't know why I'm crying," Melissa said, wiping her face frantically.

Ava scooted closer to her friend and took her hands. "Babe, you may not know why you're crying, but I do. Walter was your high school sweetheart. Everybody, including you guys, thought it was forever. It's okay to mourn the end of this thing. But you know what they say…the best way to get over someone (husbands included) is to get under—"

"Stop right there! There will be no getting under *anyone,*" Melissa said with exasperation.

Ava shook her head. "Seriously, just go out and spend time with people. People other than me. Male people… or female. You know, whatever floats your boat going forward."

Melissa didn't respond. She looked down at the papers in front of her. All signed. Her marriage to Walter was officially over. She actually was willing to try anything that would get her out of her head and stop her from thinking so much. Thinking about how some woman had messaged her to say that she had been sleeping with Walter for years and was angry because she caught Walter cheating on *them.* Melissa's initial response was that she was being pranked or that the woman was simply lying. But the woman had receipts. Before Melissa could block this slut, a flurry of illicit pictures popped up in her inbox. Along with screenshots of Walter and another mystery woman texting, arranging their next meetup. Before Melissa could even begin to process what she was looking at, she noticed the date of one of the texts. Their anniversary. The last one when Walter had been late coming home from work, forgetting the date entirely. Then he actually showered, kissed Melissa, and said he had promised his job he'd stop by some event they were hosting. He'd only be gone for an hour or two. Three tops. Melissa was pissed but also very tired of being the one to remember, plan, and think up creative ways to celebrate their anniversary and practically everything else. She made a conscious decision in that moment to just let the day pass. Walter had gotten home after she had already fallen asleep.

She had seen in that screenshot of Walter texting this girl that on their anniversary, he was texting another woman a picture of him touching himself in the shower and apologizing for running late, saying that he had to make a quick stop home to get clean and sexy for her. Walter always stayed in shape too. He was very concerned about his appearance. Never Melissa's, though. Although Melissa thought they were happy, or at least okay, she knew she wasn't the most exciting person in the world. She always thought Walter was just comfortable with her. Maybe Walter had been bored out of his fucking mind.

Once Ava was gone and Melissa was left alone with her thoughts, she pulled out her phone and downloaded the FreakyFun app. She would never admit to anyone that the thing she was most excited about was sleeping with someone else. Either Walter was extremely boring in the bedroom, or she had just gotten used to him. Melissa didn't really know which one it was, and she didn't care. She had started masturbating later in life, only really getting up the nerve to touch herself a couple of years ago. But that had been giving her more of a thrill than being with her husband. Walter was kind of a nerd. If she was being honest with herself, she never believed nerdy Walter would ever cheat on her. He'd never sent her a provocative picture in all the years she'd known him. Well, clearly maybe she didn't *know* him at all.

But now that chapter was over, and Melissa really wanted to see what other penises were like. Once her profile was created and her pictures uploaded, it took all of two minutes for Melissa to get her first message. A guy named Kurt. Kurt was in his 40s, had a shaved head, and by the looks of his profile pic, he hunted, rode a motorcycle, and smoked cigars. Melissa hated cigars, but wow, was this guy sexy. The complete opposite of Walter, who never had one hobby to speak of. Well, except the cheating. Kurt appeared to be a man's man. A real alpha male. Someone who would take control and maybe give her the pleasure of not having to think so hard for a change.

She accepted Kurt's friend request, and they began to chat immediately. He seemed articulate, interesting, and witty. And he could spell! Melissa was intrigued.

As they continued to chat and mercilessly flirt with each other, Melissa was pleasantly surprised by the fact that she didn't feel awkward at all in this new situation. And then she remembered that she was on the FreakyFun dating site, what the purpose of this whole thing was, and asked Kurt what he was looking for.

He replied: *For starters, you can call me Sir. That's a requirement.*

Melissa felt her stomach drop. While she was certainly looking for something exciting and new, a guy into dominance and requiring her to behave in a certain way just sounded like work. She didn't want any extra responsibilities. Her 9 to 5 and messy divorce had exhausted her.

Kurt had said a few other things that he was into, and although Melissa really liked his vibe, and he was undoubtedly a sexy guy, she just didn't have the bandwidth for what he was suggesting.

She left her profile up on FreakyFun but didn't engage and decided to direct her energy into getting in shape and finding a hobby that she could be passionate about.

After she got home from work the next day, she went for a jog and was pleased with how good it felt to exert her body. Melissa realized that she had really been neglecting herself. She had been last on her own list for way too long.

Kurt had continued to message her, and she found herself smiling at his banter. It was clear that he found her attractive and was still interested. He'd bluntly told her that he wanted to hold her down and fuck her hard until she screamed for mercy. Spank her, since she seemed to be terrible at following orders...and for her to call him *Sir*. She had been honest with him, that while that might possibly be exactly what she needed, it was just too much, but *maybe* in the future...

Even though she had pretty much shut down all of Kurt's advances, she still thought about him. How it might feel to be completely dominated...at another person's beck and call. To not have to give instructions to her lover, only to have him do exactly the same boring thing he always did. She pulled out her vibrator that night thinking of Kurt and came so hard it brought tears to her eyes.

About a week later, while on her customary jog at dusk, she took a new route and had an exhilarating run along a picturesque trail. She had lost a couple of pounds and was feeling a bit better about life in general. On the way back home, she smelled cigar smoke and instantly thought of Kurt. As she walked down the street, she saw the source of the smoke sitting on the steps of a brownstone. All she could really see was smoke and and his bald head.

Then the person stood up. He was wearing black, ripped jeans, a black Metallica T-shirt, and biker boots. He looked like he stepped out of some Harley Davidson ad. Although the pictures on his profile weren't the best, Melissa recognized him right away. She knew the dating site matched people based on their geography, but she had no idea Kurt was this close to her.

"Hey," he said as she approached. "I know you. Come here!"

Melissa's hair was contained in a messy bun, and she was sweaty after her run, but she was glad that she at least had on the sleek new running clothes she had recently ordered. She found her legs moving in the direction of the brownstone.

"Oh my God. Kurt? You live here?"

"Sure do. You look good. What are you doing out here?" Kurt asked her as he stood up. He had to be at least 6'4. And he was solid. Not particularly muscular, but just big... and in great shape. Melissa had to admit to herself...he looked *good.*

"Earth to the sexy brunette, *what* are you doing out here?" Kurt said as folded his arms, looking down at her with a smirk.

"I live two blocks that way," Melissa told him, pointing down the street.

"You don't say," Kurt said as he came down the stairs to approach her on the street. "If I had known that you were that close to me, I would've come to your place and taken you. Shit! Your pictures don't do you justice. You're hot as fuck."

Melissa wanted to be offended at his crude language, but she had come to enjoy it and felt her face flush.

"Is that right?" she said, trying to regain her composure. "I don't know that you wanna be telling women that you barely know that you want to kidnap them."

"Oh, I said nothing about kidnapping. I said I'd *take* you. There's a difference." Kurt came face to face with her and looked down at her with a bemused expression.

"You know," he said, and Melissa tried not to inhale whatever cologne he was wearing that went straight to her nether regions, "you ought to just come upstairs with me right now."

"Although..." Melissa cleared her throat. She actually felt lightheaded and was starting to sweat. She realized that she had never felt an attraction to anyone this way before. She had been married, and sure, she'd met attractive men, but she had an obvious wall up. She had never allowed herself to think about any man, other than her husband, in an intimate way.

"Although, I will admit, the idea does sound appealing. I'm not going upstairs with you. I already told—"

"Yeah yeah, bandwidth," Kurt said. "I get it. But the weird thing is that usually when a woman tells me she's not into it, I lose interest. Because what's she gonna do for me? I'm gonna be bored. But...it's different with you. I just want you. I wanna taste you. I wanna know how you sound when you... You know. Come upstairs. Now."

For reasons Melissa could not explain, even to herself, she followed Kurt upstairs and into his apartment.

Once inside, he didn't do the typical *this is the living room, this is the dining room* spiel. He led her through his apartment and right into the bedroom.

"You know... I could use a drink. Maybe a shower. I'm all sweaty and here you are talking about... tasting." Melissa couldn't believe she was not only in this man's apartment, she was actually considering sleeping with him. Never in a million years would she think of herself as the kind of person who would sleep with a guy the first day she met him. Well...technically she had known Kurt for weeks. This was just her first time *seeing* him in person.

"Get out of your head, kid," Kurt said, turning to her. "I can see those pretty little wheels turning, and I wanna let you know that I can assure you you will have a good time here tonight. I only want to please you. You just need to follow orders. Like a good little girl. You get that, right?"

Melissa rolled her eyes. Even though her body was betraying her by being very much aligned with whatever Kurt said, her mind was saying, *No no no!*

"Look, you're already here. Just make up your mind that you're going to enjoy yourself. Whatever happens. I like you. I may even take it easy on you.

"I—"

"Vodka okay?" Kurt asked her, ignoring the beginning of her protest and walking back toward the kitchen.

"Do you have any gin?"

Kurt smiled at her, and oh man, it was over. That smile...

How could a smile make your lady parts quiver?

"Why, of course, sexy. What kind of man would I be if I didn't have my girl's favorite drink? Gin and tonic coming right up." Kurt paused and looked at her for a moment. "Make yourself comfortable. Get out of those clothes. You can find a T-shirt in the top drawer.

Do not take a shower. Be sitting on the bed when I get back."

With that, Kurt turned around and went to the kitchen to fix her drink. Melissa kept opening and closing her mouth to say something. To let him know that she wouldn't be following his orders all night. But her body was like, *Yes, sir!*

Melissa was already tired of trying to be sensible. She decided that what her resistance boiled down to was that she didn't want to disappoint Kurt. He was looking for exciting and edgy, and she just wasn't that. Or maybe he was looking for a sub. A person that blindly followed orders. Melissa knew nothing about that life, but she was feeling far too exhausted to be subservient.

She walked over to the dresser and opened the top drawer. Kurt was surprisingly neat. Almost anally so. She didn't know why she'd expected him to be some slob, but he was the opposite of that. There were probably about two dozen white T-shirts in the drawer, perfectly folded, Gap style. She selected one and sighed to herself. She'd get out of her head for one night. She took off her sweaty clothes, put on the T-shirt and sat on the edge of the bed.

"There we go. That's my girl. Come here," Kurt said as he set the drinks on his dresser. Melissa's feet made her walk over to him. Kurt slowly put his arms around her waist and pulled her close.

"Look," Melissa said. "I—"

"Look, sexy," Kurt cut her off. "I need you to get out of your head. I don't need to hear your disclaimers. Lie down."

"Kurt..."

"Shhhh. Right here. That's right, sit here," Kurt said, directing her to lie back and put her feet up on the bed. He retrieved her drink from the dresser and handed it to her. Then he proceeded to take off his boots and pants as she sipped her drink. It was a good drink. Strong with lime, just the way she liked it. She felt the gin start to work its way down her spine and into her lower stomach, making her feel butterflies. Then the feeling worked its way down to between her legs, where gin always landed her.

"Do you want to come?" Kurt asked her, throwing her off guard.

"What? Stop. You're not roping me into your seduction techniques."

"Whatever that means... I'm about to take your hands and secure them to the headboard behind you. You will lie back and let me make you come, then wait until my next command. Is that understood?"

"Kurt..."

"It's Sir. You will call me Sir. Is that understood?"

Something about the confident, controlled way that Kurt ordered her around made her hot beyond her control. She was wet. She was almost embarrassed that she could feel the dampness between her legs.

"That's my good girl. Are you going to let me make that pussy cream?"

Melissa couldn't help but laugh. "What?"

"Lie down."

"Yes... Sir," Melissa conceded, as more of a joke than anything else, but when she saw the look on Kurt's face, her level of arousal met his instantly. She lay back on the bed, never breaking eye contact. She decided in that moment to just surrender. What did she really have to lose?

"Open your legs."

Melissa did as she was told and licked her lips seductively. Kurt barely looked at her as he grabbed her thighs and positioned her the way he wanted her. He got on his knees, grabbed her thighs, and pulled her to the edge of the bed. It felt like his mouth was everywhere all at once. He sucked her clit in between his teeth. Melissa never thought she'd enjoy such a sensation, but when she felt his teeth gently tugging at her clit, she could no longer control herself.

She was embarrassed. She had practically exploded in Kurt's face, and he lapped up every drop.

Before Melissa could utter a word, Kurt unbuckled her and threw her onto her stomach.

"Finally," Kurt said, "I get to punish you for that mouth."

Melissa had no witty comeback. While she was trying to formulate her response, she felt a quick, sharp smack on her bottom.

"Kurt!" It wasn't that it hurt. She was surprised. So surprised that she started to laugh.

Kurt popped her again. And Melissa found that the sting seemed to travel directly to her vagina. Hmmm. Could she actually get into this?

"Kurt…" Melissa said.

Kurt smacked her bottom one more time and then climbed on top of her to whisper in her ear. "It's Sir. Remember, beautiful."

The heat from Kurt's mouth tickled her ear. He turned her over onto her back and propped her up farther in the bed.

"What would you like me to do to you? What do you need, beautiful?"

"You invited me," Melissa said, gaining some of her confidence back.

"I did invite you because you're in need, and you know it," Kurt said. "Now tell me."

"I want to come," Melissa said tentatively.

Kurt ignored her, took her leg in his hand, and turned her slightly so that he could give her another smack.

"I need to cum, Sir. I *want* to come so bad." Melissa almost felt like crying. She tried to hide it because it was a weird response. She hadn't really been with anyone else except Walter. She felt her resolve melting and was actually grateful for Kurt.

"That's my good girl," Kurt said as he grabbed a condom from the nightstand and put it on. Then he opened her legs and slowly slid into her.

Melissa sucked in her breath and grabbed at the sheets on either side of her. Kurt was...not small. Or at least nothing she was used to. As he slid in and out, she could feel her body adapting to his size and beginning to enjoy it. Kurt looked at her and smiled as she closed her eyes and allowed the feeling to take over.

Melissa heard herself making sounds that had never come out of her mouth before. Kurt was making sounds that were between grunts and moans, and it only turned her on more. He reached up and placed his huge hand around her neck, squeezing gently. She was surprised that it seemed to intensify what she was feeling.

Kurt began moving faster. The man was a machine, never breaking his stride. Melissa lost it. She felt her body convulse, opening and closing on Kurt's manhood. She'd never experienced that feeling before. How was it that a veritable stranger had walked into her life and was teaching her about her own body? She opened her eyes and looked at Kurt, who was staring down at her, shaking his head.

"Fuuuuuuck," he said in a deep, guttural tone. "What the fuck!" he said as he grabbed her hands, holding them over her head as he released. "Wow."

Melissa's heart was racing as Kurt collapsed on top of her. She had finally stopped convulsing and was suddenly exhausted.

"Want some tacos? I do," Kurt said, smiling. "That was unexpected. You're something else. I like you, kid. I'm gonna clean you up, make you some food, and get you ready for the next round."

"Yes, Sir."

Chapter 8

Horny Farm Girl

by Wendy Culp

"Oh, dios mio, stop tugging at your clothes," Florencia told her friend.

"I don't know why I wore this dress," Lisa said. "And *why* I'm at this thing. This is so not me."

"You look beautiful, mami. And this is not a personality test. It's just a toy party, and it'll be fun," said Florencia. "Besides, why would I want to have a party and my best friend isn't there?"

"Because your best friend is not into *toys,*" Lisa said.

"I know, mami. I need to make some extra money and Kyla's going to show me how. It's not that I'm some freaky freaky, but she just bought a condo...from these parties, girl! And she's opened a store."

"Okay, okay. I'm here to support *you.*"

Lisa continued helping Florencia set up for the party. It was to be all woman, and each of them had been generously gifted with a $50 gift card to make a purchase. Florencia had always been very resourceful. This would probably turn out to be beneficial for her friend, and she intended to support her.

About 12 women showed up, and as they were enjoying finger foods and wine, Kyla pulled out all kinds of things from a huge pink chest that her assistant had placed in the middle of the room. The vibe was kind of like a naughty baby shower. At least that's the only reference that Lisa could think of.

She was envious of the other woman who seemed to be so comfortable holding the toys. Lisa thought she might actually faint when one of the women tried on some kind of lingerie top that had the nipples cut out. At least the woman kept on her shirt while she did it. A few of the women actually held vibrators against their bodies while nodding to each other and giving their critiques.

Yeah, this is stronger than the Rabbit. Look at the suction on that one! This edible lube is actually good.

Lisa felt completely out of her league. All she could do was giggle every time Kyla focused on her, asking her to touch or hold something. Not even Florencia knew that Lisa had never even masturbated. She had only slept with three men in her entire. But everyone was so nice, and Florencia made sure to check on her often. She actually had a good time.

As things began to wind down, Lisa said to Florencia, "See, I touched dildos, tasted lube, and let Kyla handcuff me. Aren't you proud of me?"

"Yes, I am, Mami. But! You have to buy something. You've got the $50. Spend it."

Lisa shook her head. "Oh...you take it, babe. What would I buy?"

"Just buy something, manita. I want Kyla to be impressed with the sales for tonight."

Lisa wandered around Florencia's living room, looking at the little displays Kyla had set up. The least offensive thing (in her mind) that she could find to purchase were role play cards. She still had a little money left on her card, so she snatched up a pair of sexy undies too.

When she arrived home with her brown bag of goodies, Carl looked up at her from the couch.

"How was the party?"

Lisa threw her bag in a chair and collapsed on the couch next to her husband.

"Well, I supported Flo. She's gonna be good at this stuff. The party was actually kinda fun."

Carl looked from her to the discarded bag and back. "You're not gonna show me what you got?"

"Eh, no. The only reason I bought anything at all was because Flo gave us all gift cards. For some reason, she gave me $50 to spend. I told her not to waste her money."

Carl stood up and walked over to the chair to grab the bag. "Waste? Why would it be a waste? What'd ya get?" Carl opened the bag and peered in. "Cards? They had cards? Oh, and panties. Hmmm, I like."

Lisa giggled at him. "Oh, you *like* those? Okay, I'll have to work them into the rotation.

Carl pulled the deck of cards out of the bag. "Oh, role play. Interesting... Wanna play?" he said, with a naughty grin, waving the cards at her.

"Carl..."

"Oh come on baby," Carl said with a glint in his eye. He grabbed the whiskey from their bar and poured each of them a shot.

"Whiskey? I can't drink whiskey," Lisa said. "I thought you would find this hilarious. I didn't think you'd actually be interested."

Carl ran his fingers through his blond hair, looking her up and down. "I am in love with my wife. You're beautiful. Why in the hell wouldn't I want to indulge with you?"

Lisa appreciated her husband's appraisal. They were a good match. Both were pretty conservative but not uptight. She knew Carl found her attractive and even called her sexy at times, but she didn't quite think of herself that way.

"You know what turns me on about this?" Carl asked.

Lisa shook her head.

Carl walked over and pulled her up from the couch, encircling her in his arms. "What I love is that I know what a sweet woman you are. You're my innocent baby, and when you get naughty, it just does something to me. You remember the last time I gave you that shot of tequila?"

Lisa closed her eyes and sighed. "I don't even want to think about that night. I was throwing up the whole next day."

"Well, I'm not suggesting that you drink as much as you did that night. But my point is that we had a great time! You were a wild woman."

Lisa laughed. "I wouldn't go that far, but I hear you, husband."

Carl clapped his hands and handed her a shot. They toasted each other, and Lisa attempted to get the entire shot down her throat without gagging. She felt the liquid burning its way down through her chest. Her eyes watered, and Carl laughed as he quickly took his shot and ripped open the bag and pulled the cards out. He placed the deck on the coffee table. "Okay, who's first?"

Lisa took a deep breath and felt herself start to loosen up. "I guess I'll go first." Lisa kicked off her shoes and walked over to the table to pull her first card.

"Horny farm girl? That's not too bad."

Carl pulled his card. "Escaped convict," he read, laughing.

Lisa and Carl just looked at each other and burst out laughing again. "Look, if we're gonna do this thing, we're gonna have to stop giggling."

"Okay, okay!" Lisa said, trying to straighten her face into a serious expression. "Well, what does it say the horny farm girl is supposed to do?"

"It's role play, baby. We'll have to come up with a scenario. Okay," Carl said, clapping his hands again and then arranging his face into a snarl.

"What is that?" Lisa said cracking up. "Is that your *convict* face?"

"Look, stop making me laugh. I'm gonna go outside and knock on the door. You'll let me in, and I'll take it from there."

Lisa thought about Florencia and how proud she would be of her friend at this moment. She couldn't believe Carl was so invested in this. She shrugged and said, "Okay, let's do it."

Carl immediately ran outside as Lisa smiled to herself and shook her head. She couldn't believe they were actually doing this! Her husband never ceased to amaze her.

Carl knocked on the door and Lisa opened it, leaning against the doorjamb.

"Yeah?" she said in her most country accent.

Carl stifled a grin and said, "Ma'am, I hate to bother you, but I've gotten myself into a bad situation. I need a place to hide for the night. May I stay in your barn?"

"Why should I let you stay in my barn? You look dangerous."

"Ma'am, I assure you, I would be of no danger to you. I really need your help."

Lisa folded her arms. "What's in it for me?"

Escaped convict Carl slowly came into the house, closing the door behind him. "If you pull that dress up, I can make it worth your while, ma'am."

"Pull up my dress? What's that gotta do witchu stayin' in my barn?"

Carl giggled but composed himself immediately. "Let me earn my keep."

"I don't know. You could be a killer. A sexy killer, but a killer just the same. I'm scared," Lisa said.

Carl reached out and took her hand. "I'm no killer, ma'am. There's just a big misunderstanding. I'd be mighty grateful."

"Hmmm. Okay. The barn is this way," Lisa said as she led her husband to the guest bedroom. "This is real kind of you, ma'am. This is real nice. You gonna let me thank you?"

"You do seem mighty grateful. What you got in mind?"

Escaped convict Carl picked Lisa up and threw her on the bed. "I got a thang for farm girls, ma'am. They got the tastiest pussies this side of the Mississippi."

"Well, you better make it good if you tryin' to stay the whole night," Lisa said as she raised her dress up a tiny bit.

Carl walked over and raised the dress up to her waist. He looked down at Lisa as if he'd never seen her before. He slowly slid her panties off and threw them to the side.

"Ma'am, may I please taste it? It looks so good."

In spite of herself, Lisa was aroused. She almost felt like a different person. Like a horny farmgirl. "Yeah, you can taste."

Carl got on his knees at the end of the bed and pulled Lisa to the edge. He slowly inserted a finger. "Ma'am, is your pussy always this wet?" He pulled his finger out and sucked it. He then slid in two fingers, slowly going in and out. Carl moaned and spread her legs even wider. He pulled her closer, practically burying his face between her legs and stuck his tongue inside of her, moaning like it was his last meal.

Lisa didn't even have a response for him. She couldn't remember Carl ever doing something like that. She closed her eyes and concentrated on the sensation happening between her legs.

"Mmmm, it's so good, ma'am," Carl said, smacking his lips. He took his fingers and spread her open. His long tongue seemed to find a little groove and up and down Carl licked rhythmically.

Lisa began to feel a building up in her stomach that spread to her thighs and then all over her body. She grabbed Carl's head and begged him not to stop. She'd never felt this before. It was like she had stuck her finger in an electrical socket.

Just when she felt like she was about to explode, Carl simultaneously pushed her back and climbed onto the bed on top of her. "Ma'am, I need to feel you. This is the way I can earn my keep. Can I make love to you?"

"Yes. Yes!"

Carl slid into her and moaned. "Oh, it's sooo wet. Mmmm."

As he continued pumping into her, hitting Lisa in a spot she didn't know she had, she finally released and Carl grabbed her waist, pushing himself even farther into her.

"Oh my God, OH!"

"Yes, baby! Let it go. That's it."

"Carl! Oh God, Carl," Lisa screamed as she orgasmed harder than she ever had before. She looked up at Carl with big eyes, almost in disbelief that she was actually experiencing this feeling.

As she began to calm down, Carl pulled out of her and turned her around. He pulled her waist up and positioned himself behind her. He slid into her easily, and Lisa was surprised that she felt an entirely different sensation. It was as if the role play, and maybe pretending to be someone else had allowed her to access a new level of arousal.

"Shit, this feels incredible, ma'am. I sure do appreciate you letting me earn my keep. Maybe you'll let me stay another night?"

Lisa had no words. She felt like she was losing control. "Mmmm. Ohhhhh. Omigod, omigod. Carl!"

She grabbed at the pillow above her head and buried her face into it.

"No," Carl said hoarsely, pulling the pillow away from her and pushing into her even harder. "Let me see you, baby. You're so sexy."

Lisa looked back at Carl as she orgasmed again. His eyes were half-mast, and he looked like he was in ecstasy. That took Lisa over the top. She arched her back and pushed Carl even deeper into her as she orgasmed again. She felt Carl grip her waist even tighter.

"Oh shit, baby. Yes," Carl moaned breathlessly as he shot hot and fast into his wife. "Oh my fucking God."

Carl collapsed on the bed next to Lisa, and she turned over on her side to face him.

"Well, I guess you can stay for tonight," Lisa said. "Now get in there and fix me up something to eat."

Carl burst into laughter as he pulled his wife into his arms. "Ready to pull another card?"

Chapter 9

Hometown Girl
by Cynthia Urban

"Girl! I'm actually gonna miss you!" Ciara told Christina as they both sat on her suitcase to get it to close.

Christina smiled at her roommate. "Why do you sound surprised?"

"Your little innocent, lily white ass. You walked in here like you were straight from some kind of Mormon camp," Ciara said as she unplugged her phone charger from the wall and threw it into her bag. She did a final look around the room, seemingly satisfied that she wasn't forgetting anything.

"Why do all of your references about white people involve Mormons? I've never even met a Mormon," Christina said, laughing.

"Cuz...all I did was watch that reality show about those Mormon people breaking free before I came here. I loved that shit. The only white people I saw in fucking rural Mississippi were...well, none."

Christina shook her head at her roommate. Ciara was endlessly entertaining. She had been a great roommate this first semester, and Christina would miss her terribly...but she was completely distracted.

She'd be going back home to Naperville, Illinois where she was sure she would run into her ex-boyfriend, Keith.

It felt weird to even label or think of Keith as her ex. That sounded way too final and too adult to her. She still loved him. She'd probably always love him. She knew he loved her. But they had never slept together, and Christina knew that they had been moving in that direction. Well, at least Keith had. He'd been trying to broach the subject with her in a variety of ways. But Christina wanted to figure out how she felt before she was upfront and honest with Keith.

While she obviously loved him (they had been a couple all throughout her high school years!) and did want to sleep with him, she knew there was no way he could remain committed to her while he was at the University of Michigan and she was at Northwestern. Keith was a catch. Tall, handsome, athletic, and smart. Christina knew the girls would be beating down his door. While she trusted him implicitly, she just didn't want the added pressure of a long-distance relationship. Surely, there would be tons of women more exciting than her. She would be devastated to receive that phone call from Keith one day saying that maybe they should see other people. She had believed, with every fiber of her being, that was what her future held, so she basically decided to beat Keith to the punch.

"My little Chrissy Wissy! I'm gonna miss you. You're the first white girl I've ever been friends with, and I love you!"

"CC!" laughed Christina. "I love you too. But it's only a week!"

"Okay, okay. I may have attachment issues, but that's another story for another day. I'm working through it."

Ciara and Christina hugged each other one final time before walking off in separate directions. Even Ciara had told her that it was crazy to walk away from a perfectly wonderful guy and a perfectly wonderful relationship for no reason. Christina had begun to regret her decision almost as soon as she made it. And certainly after a few weeks and experiencing what the average college guy was like, she knew she'd made a mistake.

But she also knew that a guy like Keith would not just wander around campus unnoticed. He would be a hot commodity, and what was going to keep him committed to his virgin girlfriend, whose favorite thing in the world to do was buy a new book? She couldn't compete. So part of her reasoning for the break-up was so that Keith could go out into the world unencumbered and sleep with whatever skank he wanted to.

That really wasn't fair. Christina didn't really believe it would be a skank to deflower Keith. It would probably be a devastatingly hot physics major or something. Maybe a Michigan cheerleader...

Christina shook her head as a text came through from her dad, telling her that he was outside waiting. She grabbed her bags, walked out into the sunshine, and made her way to her dad's truck.

Christina was a Daddy's girl. He grabbed her into a big bear hug and spun her around.

"Dad!" Christina said, mortified.

"I can't show my baby girl how much I miss her? Get in here," he said, opening the passenger door for her. He loaded her things into the trunk, and they began their trek home.

"You know I could've just Ubered, Dad. It's only an hour."

"Nope. I want the full experience of picking my kid up for her fall break. You're all I got. You gave me prom, graduation...college. All the experiences. Your idiot brother so far is only giving me a coronary."

"What's Charlie up to now?"

"Not a damn thing," her father said, exasperated. "He somehow flunked out of his arts and sciences program, and he's in the basement *depressed*. I don't think we're ever gonna get rid of him. You kids! You're not exactly off the hook either. Your mother literally said to me, as I was walking out the door, *'Don't ask her about Keith.'* Now, pumpkin. What's that supposed to mean?"

Christina sank down in her seat. Her parents were hilarious. "Dad...if she said not to ask me about... Keith, then why is that the first thing you did?"

"Oh, don't act surprised. I always do the exact opposite of what your mother tells me to do. Now, what's going on with you two?" her father said, glancing at her with concern.

She wanted to put her dad at ease. She knew he loved Keith like his own son. "It's no big deal, Dad. We just took a break, that's all. I didn't want to say anything before I left because I just wanted to concentrate on *not* flunking out, e.g., Charles Caldwell II. I knew you'd probably take it harder than Keith, so I only told Mom a couple of weeks ago because she kept asking about him. I haven't even talked to him."

"Pumpkin," her dad said, coming to a red light and turning to face her. "You haven't talked to Keith since you left. That was months ago. You two have been joined at the hip since you were what, 12? How do you not talk to your best friend?"

Christina stared straight ahead and sat perfectly still to try and prevent the tears from escaping her eyes and streaming down her face. She did not want to cry in front of her father. She didn't need this right now. "Dad, can we just drive? I can't talk about this right now."

One thing she loved about her dad was that he was very open and upfront about his feelings on any topic, but if you weren't quite ready to explore that topic with him, he'd leave you alone. He would not leave her alone if she started to cry, though. So she fought off the tears and looked out the window, changing the subject.

Once back home and in her childhood bedroom, Christina missed Keith even more. She had changed her mind about attempting to avoid him. That would cause more trouble than it was worth with how close both of their families were.

Sure enough, just as Christina had finished unpacking her things, her mother appeared in the doorway to say that a few people were stopping by for an impromptu BBQ.

"Mom..."

"Oh, Tina. You're going to have to see him at some point..."

Three hours later, as she was bringing her dad and uncle fresh beers, Keith and his parents came walking into the back yard. The parents all went their own way, talking about the new deck her dad had built and whatever else old people talked about. Keith walked directly up to her.

Christina had no idea what to say to him. Part of her wanted to remain in the unknown. This moment before he opened his mouth and told her that his girl-friend was in the car...or he was engaged...or he had a baby on the way.

Okay, admittedly, all of those things were ridiculous, mostly. But she had never been guilty of having an underactive imagination.

"Aren't you gonna say hello?"

"Hi," Christina said awkwardly.

"Tina," Keith said and pulled her in close for a hug. He smelled as good as he looked. He had put on a few pounds. Apparently, all muscle. His hair was longer, and he had allowed himself to grow a beard. He looked good. Really good. "God, I've missed you."

"You have?"

Keith stared at her for a second. "What? Of course! You kinda left me high and dry."

Christina rolled her eyes. "I wouldn't quite describe it that way."

Keith continued staring. His eyes took in her hair, which was also longer, flowing down her back, instead of in its customary hair tie. He lingered over her collarbone, her breasts, her hips...all the way down to the new sandals Ciara had picked out for her.

"You look incredible, you know that?"

Christina huffed and blushed against her will.

"No, I mean it. I love your hair that way, and you've... what is it? You've gained weight."

"Keith! You don't say that to a person. A girl, anyway."

"Shit, why not? You look like a woman. I mean, it's only been a few weeks, but the weight...trust me, it's in all the right places. You look great, Tina."

"Thank you, Keith." Christina closed her eyes briefly and took a deep breath. "So...tell me, I bet you've got a girlfriend already. What's she like?"

Keith almost choked on his bottle of water. "A girlfriend?"

"Yes, a girlfriend. I know you're a man...with needs."

"Tina, don't be ridiculous. Yes, I've met a ton of girls. All kinds of girls. Tall ones...short ones...funny ones... serious ones..."

Christina punched his arm playfully. Just touching him sent shivers all over her body, and she realized what she wanted to do.

"Be serious," she told him.

"Tina, there's no one like *you*. I know you thought you were being super mature to break it off before we went off to college, like in one of your romance novels. But this isn't that. I love you. I will never want anyone but you. You may have thought that you broke up with me, and it was a done deal, but I didn't accept it."

"You didn't accept it? What are you talking about?"

"I refuse to be broken up with. You're still my woman... in my head," Keith said, looking down at his feet sheepishly.

"Wait here, okay? I'll be right back," Christina told Keith.

She went into the house and grabbed some of the throw blankets scattered around the living room. She went and threw them into her dad's truck and let him know that she and Keith had to make a run. He was in full grill master mode and waved her off with an approving smile. Before she made her way back to

Keith, Christina grabbed a big bag of chips, a couple of Solo cups, and a bottle of 1800.

She put the goodies in the trunk and got Keith's attention. She beckoned for him to sneak away and join her in the truck.

Keith theatrically tiptoed through the backyard and out to the street where she was waiting for him. Once he was in, and she pulled off, he looked in the back seat and saw the blankets.

"Okay...a picnic?"

"Not exactly," Christina said cryptically.

She took the service road that led to Forest Park woods and drove about five minutes into a secluded section.

Keith seemed to be quieter than usual. Probably trying to figure out what she was up to.

Their thighs touched in her father's old truck, and the sensation was a new one for her. She had really missed Keith.

She put the truck in park and asked Keith to grab the goods out of the trunk. He looked at her questioningly but did as he was told.

"Yeeeeah," he said when he popped the trunk and spotted the tequila. "My girl has grown way the fuck up," he said, laughing.

"Oh, shut up. We've had shots before," Christina said.

"Yeah, but never from tequila *stolen* from your parents. You're a bad girl," Keith said with a tone that penetrated something deep inside.

She took the bottle from him and poured them both a drink. "Here's to our first semester of college. Look at us."

Keith didn't look excited about the toast and put his cup down into the cupholder.

"What's wrong? You don't want it?"

"Are you trying to break up with me again? Like... more formally or something this time, because..."

Christina took his cup and handed it back to him as she sipped her own. "I'm not breaking up with you. I miss you."

Keith put his cup down again at her words. "I miss you too."

"Please take a drink. I don't wanna drink alone. I'm nervous enough as it is," Christina said as she glanced at the blankets in the backseat.

"Nervous? So you *are* trying to break up with me again. Or tell me something. Do *you* have a boyfriend?"

"Would you stop?" Christina said earnestly. "I made a mistake. I want you. There's no one else for me. I know you could have so many more exciting girls, and I just didn't want you to feel trapped... and—"

Keith finally took a big gulp of his tequila and put the cup down again. He took one of her hands in his and kissed it. He looked at Christina thoughtfully.

"You know...the minute I got on campus, somebody came to my room and told me that there was a party. And I was like, *Hell yeah, here we go.* All I was thinking about was being able to hang out and party with the bros without having to worry about the parentals. But the moment I sat foot in this party, there were half-naked, drunk girls everywhere. I wasn't even there for an hour, and this girl takes me by the hand and pulls me into this room. She starts taking off her clothes and I'm like, *I don't even know you.*" Keith took a deep breath and looked into Christina's eyes. "I could've slept with that girl that night. I could probably sleep with a new girl every day. But I don't want them. I have been waiting for my actual girlfriend to come to her senses."

With that, Christina put her drink down and reached up to run her fingers through Keith's hair. She pulled him to her and finally kissed the lips that had haunted her dreams for weeks.

She felt Keith inhale deeply before he practically pulled her into his lap, deepening their kiss.

"How in the hell could you think that I'd want anyone who isn't you?" Keith said, finally coming up for air.

"I knew you wanted more," Christina said timidly. "I was scared to...give you that...more. Only to have you go off and be a big football star and forget all about me."

"That," Keith said, raising her chin to meet her eyes, "is impossible."

Christina looked at the back seat and then at Keith. She climbed to the back and spread the blankets out. She then pulled her dress up and removed her panties, while smiling at Keith's shocked face.

"Tina...you don't have to feel like..."

"I want to. I've wanted to for a very, very long time."

"I can wait forever for you, if that's what you really want," Keith said, although his eyes were glued to Christina's golden thighs.

"I don't know how you're a straight A student. You're not a very good listener. Get back here."

Keith climbed into the back, glancing all around at the deserted woods. He frantically began unbuckling his belt and Christina helped him get out of his pants.

Once Keith was out of his pants, he wrapped a blanket around him and looked at Christina again. "Are you sure, Tina?"

"Keith!"

He didn't need to be told again. He looked down at his sweet, beautiful girlfriend and showered her with kisses. Her earlobe, her neck. Keith unbuttoned the top buttons of her dress and let his lips linger on her chest, breathing in her scent.

He reached around her back, unfastening her bra. Christina closed her eyes and sighed as she felt Keith's hot mouth encircle her nipple. She had fantasized about this moment dozens of times.

"You smell so good. You're so soft," Keith said as he flicked her other nipple with his tongue before seemingly taking the whole thing into his mouth. Christina loved this sensation. In the past, she had always pushed Keith away at a certain point, when they were making out because she didn't want him to get too excited when they both knew it couldn't go anywhere. She didn't even know what she had been waiting for. When she was younger, she used to say that she was waiting until marriage. When she got a little older, she was just waiting for the perfect time, and that had never seemed to come. Keith always respected her wishes and had stopped pressuring her, but the desire was always there.

There was no reason to wait. He was the man of her dreams. And if she had waited all this time for the perfect person and situation, and for some reason, it turned out *not* to be Keith...Well, she would be perfectly content with the fact that he had been her first. There was no one else in the world that she would rather give herself to.

As if reading her mind, Keith had begun to position himself between her legs.

"Tina, I have been dreaming of this moment. You're my girl. I love you so much. I'm serious when I say I will *never* want anyone but you."

She felt him at her opening, and her heart started to race. She hadn't actually thought about how this might feel. Would it hurt? She had never talked about the first time with anyone.

"Are you okay?"

Christina opened her legs wider. She was ready. She nodded at Keith to keep going.

He slowly inserted the head, and she felt okay. Keith looked down at her as he began to breathe faster. "Oh Tina. Wow," he said and closed his eyes.

Christina felt a sharp pain. Or more like she was being stretched open. She felt like a new toy that had never been played with, and she very much wanted to move past that feeling.

She didn't have to wait long because Keith went a little deeper, watching her reaction carefully. That move did something different for Christina. It felt good.

"Oh, I like that. Mmmm," she said, closing her eyes and relaxing into the moment. So *this* was what Ciara was always on about. She got it now.

"You like it? It feels good?" Keith said excitedly.

"Yes. Oh, go slow. Yessss," Christina said hoarsely.

"Ahhhh, yes. This feels too good."

Keith alternated between staring at her in disbelief and closing his eyes, trying to maintain control. He kept his slow, steady pace, and Christina could feel herself growing wetter. She did not at all expect to enjoy her first time, but this felt amazing. What the hell had she been waiting for?

She reached up and slid her hands into Keith's hair and began moving with him. She was enjoying this. And she knew there was no one on this planet she could be like this with.

"Keith...Keith," Christina moaning, reaching some sort of peak.

"Baby, shit!" Keith said as he quickly pulled out and spilled all over her stomach.

He hung his head down in mock shame. "Why'd you have to go calling my name? Fuck. Wow!"

He used one of the smaller blankets to clean Christina off as she smiled up at him. "Your mom's gonna kill you about her blankets. That woman loves a throw."

Christina laughed. "This is true. You know...I'm really glad that we got to know each other first," Christina said as Keith snuggled beside her in the back seat.

"Oh? Why's that?" Keith said, still catching his breath.

"Because all I want to do is *that!* All day, every day. Oh my God! How are we gonna make this work?"

"Woman, it's only a five-hour drive. I don't care. I'll walk for that lovin'. We'll make it work, okay? If we can wait years...what's a few weeks here and there?"

Christina sighed and wrapped her arms around her boyfriend's neck. "Round 2? Gimme that tequila!"

Chapter 10

The New Girl at Work

by James Lafayette

"That's a very cool T-shirt," I said to the girl standing in front of me. I believed in the power of 3s. This was the third time I had seen her, and she happened to be wearing a shirt featuring a character from my current favorite anime show. I'd been in this predicament before. There was the edgy looking girl on the 9th floor that was wearing a cool vintage tee, and when I made a joke about the character on her shirt, she rolled her eyes and said that it was just some crap shirt that her ex-boyfriend had left at her apartment. She knew nothing of anime and immediately seemed to judge me for having an interest.

Girls here were different. I was born and raised in New York City. My family had moved around just about every two years. I'd lived all over Brooklyn and Queens in great neighborhoods and some not so great. The thing that I loved the most was the diversity. Although it was currently the politically correct thing to say that you were all about equity and diversity, I had grown up with virtually every ethnicity, race, and religion surrounding me at home and at school; it was all I knew. And I felt like a fish out of water with virtually hundreds of carbon copies of me inhabiting Silicon Valley. Sure, Enigma was *the* place to be. Everyone wanted a stint here on their resume because you could write your own checks after that, but on some days, I felt like I was dying a slow death.

I remembered when they gave me the initial tour, during my first interview. There were the foosball and pool tables that had become the tech bro standard. Then there were the copious snack rooms, the elaborate coffee bar, the VR room, ball pit, bowling alley and beers on Thursdays. There was everything a person could ever want and need, without ever having to leave the building. You could practically live in the building because when you got tired, there were also *nap rooms*. It was great. I loved everything about the place. I would've probably shit myself ten years ago at 21, but I'd pretty much gotten used to the culture, and it was all becoming old news to me. This building did have something that I had *not* experienced before, though. And that was the omelet making robot. Now that was a thing of beauty. Perfect omelets every time, and I was a sucker for a good omelet.

Ironically, no one seemed to have much interest in the omelet bar. Maybe people hadn't discovered it yet. Maybe omelets were only cool to me... Whatever the reason it was mostly deserted, I didn't care. I was grateful that there was never really a line. Except this new girl. She seemed to be into the omelet station too.

Mystery girl turned around and smirked at me. "Thank you" was all she said, then she turned back around and entered the ingredients for her omelet onto the digital screen.

"I've pretty much seen it all," I said to her. "But this has impressed me. These omelets are amazing, right?"

She turned fully around, and I almost lost it. She was about 5'7 and mocha-skinned with the sexiest eyes I'd ever seen. The term *bedroom eyes* popped into my head, and I immediately tried to shake that thought away. She was curvy but in an athletic way. And she had curly brown hair that was currently in a pouf on top of her head. She wore black Clark Kent-type glasses and had four tiny gold hoops in each ear, a tiny lotus tattoo behind one ear, and what looked to be the wing of a phoenix on the part of her arm that was exposed. She wore skinny jeans and Retro 1s.

"I was wondering who I'd have to sleep with around here to get a good omelet," she said deadpan.

"Uh..."

"Kidding. Please close your mouth," mystery woman said with a smirk. "Denise."

"Huh?" I said, momentarily dazzled by her smile.

"I'm Denise," she said, nodding. No doubt to encourage me to act like a normal human being.

"Oh. I'm Matt," I said as I went in for a handshake, and she just kind of lifted her chin to acknowledge me. "Where'd you get that shirt? I've never seen a Chopper shirt. Maybe Luffy...but never Chopper."

"My brother actually made it for me for my last birthday," Denise said as she grabbed her completed omelet. "He's in school for animation right now, so I get very cool gifts."

"That is very cool," I said. "I might have to bug you for your brother's contact info. I want a custom shirt for my birthday too!"

"Hold on there. I don't just let anyone have access to baby bro. I'll have to make sure you're cool first."

"Oh, I'm cool," I said as I reached for my completed omelet. "Cooler than the other side of the pillow."

"Oh! Well, that settles it," Denise said facetiously. "Ladies and gentlemen, I present...Matt. The coolest guy in town." With a fake bow and flourish, Denise headed toward the elevator.

"Hey!" I said, running after her like a moron. "Since you're so cool and everything and I'm obviously cool, maybe I can buy your next omelet or maybe lunch from the cafeteria?"

"As tempting as *that* sounds... if we can make it Korean BBQ for dinner, then I'm in."

I felt my eyes widen in surprise. Was this girl actually giving me the time of day? And she liked Korean BBQ!

"Yes! Name the time and place and I'm there!"

"Seven-thirty tomorrow night. Meet me at Gooyi Gooyi. It's two blocks that way," Denise said, pointing with her chin. "Their banchan are next level," she added as she winked and stepped into the elevator.

To say I was smitten would sound like a ridiculous thing my sister would say. But that's how I felt. Denise was hot! And sexy. And very clearly smart as fuck if she worked here. I didn't know one thing about her, other than she liked anime, probably cool gym shoes, and Korean BBQ. Oh, and she had a brother that did animation. Okay, so I knew four things about her. I stuck my chest out with pride. I was pleased with myself. Even with my limited knowledge, she was already the coolest woman I'd met since moving to California.

"Yo, ping pong tournament starting at two in the lounge, bro. See you there?" I turned around and saw Aidan pouring his third cold brew of the day.

"Absolutely not," I said as I headed to the elevator.

"I never know if you're being sarcastic, bro. I love it," Aidan said laughing. I shrugged at him as the elevator doors closed and he continued to point at me and shake his head. Like he couldn't figure me out since I'd never played any pool, golf, ping pong, or anything else all of my colleagues seemed to be obsessed with. Maybe I was getting old.

"How long have you worked for Enigma?" I asked Denise over dinner the next night.

"It's only been three weeks or so. How 'bout you?"

"About three months. I'm surprised I haven't seen you around more," I said.

"Well, I've kinda been swamped since my first day, to be honest," Denise said. "It's ironic that there is every kind of distraction under the sun here, but you never have time to indulge, you know?"

"Exactly. Yet there are some guys who always seem to fit in a ping pong game. I don't know how they do it."

"Not a lover of ping pong?" Denise asked as she dipped a short rib into sauce. "I'd pegged you as the ping pong champ."

"Really? Is it the blond hair?"

"Yep. Along with the hoodie, flip-flops, and utility backpack."

"I do not, nor have I ever owned a pair of flip-flops," I told her, shaking my head. "You have clearly racially profiled me."

Denise laughed. "You're going there?" She looked under the table at my shoes. "Okay, I stand corrected. Thank God. I think I would've left this table if I peeped a pair of orthopedic flip flops. How is it that you live in California and you don't own a pair of flip-flops?"

"I've only been here for a few months," I told her. "I haven't been fully indoctrinated."

"Oh, really? Where are you from?"

"I'm originally from New York. By way of Brooklyn and Queens."

"Ohhhhh," Denise said, raising an eyebrow. "That's why you stand out."

"Well, you definitely stand out," I told her shyly. "In the best way. Are you from here?"

"No sir. I'm from Atlanta. But I just graduated from the University of DC, so here am I getting used to yet another new place."

"The University of DC! That's the best computer science program at any HBCU. Impressive!"

"Hold the fucking phone," Denise said, tossing her chopsticks down. "How the hell would you...did you know that?"

"I went to Howard," I told her.

"The fuck you did."

I smiled. I liked this girl. "Okay...my best friend did. I *loved* visiting him. I was there as much as I could be."

"Ohhhh. So you find Black culture fascinating? Are you like our colleagues at work who like to invite me out so that they can feel good about themselves? Feel like they're being *inclusive.*"

"First of all," I told her, folding my arms, "*you* invited *me* out. Secondly, I don't believe anyone asking you out is doing anything out of the goodness of their heart. You're stunning. I'm sure guys are beating down your door."

Denise threw her head back and laughed. Today, her curls were free and gloriously wild. I noticed that she had shades of golden brown mixed in there. I wondered vaguely what it would feel like to immerse my hands into that hair.

"Have you not met our colleagues? No one is beating down my door. They're all just trying to figure out how much of a bitch I am. Because of course being a Black woman who knows her stuff, takes no shit, and is not easily intimidated is gonna be a bitch. But nope. No date requests just yet."

"Then our colleagues are bigger idiots than I thought," I said, pausing briefly before I said, "So, this is a date then?"

"Do you want it to be?" Denise said flirtatiously.

"Hell yeah! Are you kidding me?"

Denise seemed to size me up. "Let's go next door and get a real drink."

I was already up and pulling out her chair out. "Let's."

Denise laughed as she stood up, brushing against me as she stepped away from her seat.

She smelled like heaven. I instantly thought of the time I was in Vegas and walked into my first casino. The thing I noticed was the smell. It was a cross between a really classy hotel and a strip club. It was intoxicating. My dad had told me that the scent was supposed to be addictive to get you to stay and gamble longer. That's what Denise smelled like.

After we had a couple of shots and a couple more drinks at the bar, Denise had opened up a bit and shared more about herself. As I suspected, she loved anime—not so much gym shoes. The retro Jordans had been a gift. She played tennis competitively. Hence the incredible body. She painted in oils, and she played the drums. I had to do everything in my power not to continue to picture her naked on the drums.

"Do you have a set of drums at home? Like, are you in an apartment somewhere?"

"I'm very lucky. My dad bought me a condo when I graduated. It's in the perfect spot, far enough away from neighbors where I can make all the noise I want. I keep my drums in the garage, though. I turned one of my spare bedrooms into an art studio, basically."

"You might just be the most interesting person in the world. Drums...painting... and *tennis*? How'd you ever get into tennis?"

"Why do you seem so shocked? Have you not met a Black person that plays tennis?"

"Well...no," I said. "Actually, I don't know anyone that plays tennis. You're just way too sophisticated for me."

"Whatever," Denise said, smiling at me. "Don't be alarmed, but I also love documentaries. It's like my favorite thing to do, when I have time."

For some reason unbeknownst to me, Denise continued to hang out with me. She was a tiny bit correct. Even though I had dated Black girls before, she was different from any of them. But she was actually just different from any girl I'd dated. She definitely had a chip on her shoulder and continued to poke fun at and challenge me whenever I was surprised by something she revealed about herself.

She was only 25. That was another reason she continued to catch me off guard. I tried to remember my frame of mind at that age, and even though it was only six years ago, I felt like an entirely different person. I'd been a boy for my entire twenties. Now I felt like a man. Denise was all woman and seemed like she had always been.

I sat on Denise's bed, surrounded by pillows and scarves and all things bohemian and watched her as she configured her Meta Quest for us to play together. I couldn't believe I was actually in her condo...in her bedroom. In her bed! We had been out three times, and this was the first time she'd invited me back to her place. All I wanted to do was pull her into the bed with me and find out what that smooth, chocolate skin tasted like, but I was petrified to turn her off. I couldn't figure out if she was just a good girl who didn't do *that* on the first date. Or the second or the third. OR if she was just still trying to figure me out.

So here I sat on the bed, ramping up for a riveting game of VR tennis, since it happened to be midnight and there was no place to play in person.

"I can't believe you never played before," she said, turning to me. "I promise you, this is going to feel so real that you will be a pro by the time we make it to a real court. I'll be in the living room, and you can be in here."

"We can't play in the same room?"

"No! You've never done this before?" Denise said, her voice muffled before she disappeared into her closet.

"I'm afraid to disappoint you, but no ma'am."

"Oh, you are in for a treat, my friend," Denise said as she reemerged in an actual tennis dress. "Don't look at me like that. I get hot when I play, and my glasses fog up in the headset."

I raised my eyebrows, trying to formulate a suitable response. Denise's black and white tennis dress was tiny. It was obvious she wasn't wearing a bra. I couldn't take my eyes off her. She probably had the prettiest legs I'd ever seen. They were long and toned, like a supermodel. I wanted so badly to pull that dress up and see more.

"Earth to Matt," Denise was saying slowly. I watched her eyes watch my eyes take in her appearance appreciatively. She smiled.

"I'm sorry, D. You know I'm attracted to you. I've been trying very hard to be good. But fuck, man. That dress?"

"The tennis does it for you?" she said, smiling. She slowly walked over to me, and I stood up, facing her.

She put her arms around my neck, looking up at me. "Who the fuck told you to be good?"

I kissed her. She tasted exactly like I thought she would. Indescribable. I caressed her waist and ran my hand over her hips and finally her butt. She was incredibly soft. I had never in my life wondered what it would feel like to cuddle with someone. Until this moment. I reached up and rubbed her back. Then her neck.

Denise reached up and cupped my face, pulling me closer and moaning into my mouth. That did it. I was as hard as a rock, and I knew she felt it.

I caressed her back, then her hair. It was so soft. Just like everything else about her. I wanted to touch the front of her body as well but didn't want to come off too eager.

Denise's hands were in my hair as she pushed her body up against mine. I couldn't take it anymore. I reached down and cupped her ass, only to discover that she had nothing on under her dress. I abruptly pulled away and looked at her in shock.

"What? Girls need love too," she said, laughing. She stepped away from me and pulled the dress over her head. Sexy, pear-shaped breasts with tiny brown nipples stared at me. As well as a beautiful bush of curly brown hair between her legs. Now *that* was different. I could not find a woman my age that actually had pubic hair. I knew I was staring at this woman like a pervert, but fuck. She was sexy as hell.

Denise cocked her head at me.

"You're fucking beautiful. I'm sorry. I'm dumbfounded. Wow," I said, removing my clothes as fast as I could.

I walked over to Denise and gently pushed her back until she was sitting on the edge of her bed. She scooted back until she was in the middle, and I climbed next to her. We kissed again, and I could swear the second time was even better. This girl was an amazing kisser. I reached down and caressed her breasts. I decided to begin having a mental conversation with my penis at that time. *Please do not come too fast. Please do not come too fast.*

"Matt," Denise said, pulling away from me. "This isn't just some fad kind of thing, is it? Like a box to check.... Fuck a Black chick..."

"I told you, I've dated Black girls before. *And* white ones. I think there was one Asian..."

Denise laughed. "Oh, really?"

I reached over her and grabbed my phone off her nightstand. "Look," I said, opening up my IG to show her pics of my ex. My blonde-haired, blue-eyed ex.

Denise grabbed my phone. "Oh, a blonde? How do you go from a blonde to me?"

"Cuz I'm not into blondes."

"Well, you dated one."

"I liked her in spite of the blond hair," I said.

"Hmmm," Denise said skeptically.

"I'm into smart, funny, interesting, witty...sexy women. You are exquisite. I'm into *you.*"

I guess I answered correctly because she straddled me and kissed me again. I inhaled her sweet fragrance and touched her everywhere, no longer hesitant.

Denise pulled away from the kiss again, this time to grab a condom from her nightstand. She looked me in the eyes as she slid it onto me. And then *she* slid onto me. I briefly begged my penis to not embarrass me as Denise slowly rode me. It was erotic and sensual. The lights were on, and she looked at me. Unashamed and with total confidence. Unlike most of the women I'd been with.

It felt so good that I knew I'd lose it soon. I grasped Denise around the waist and placed her on her back. I took control and was inside her once again. Although I had a little more control and just maybe I could last longer, it was still a struggle. She felt incredible.

She reached behind her head and grabbed the head-board, pulling her legs from around my waist and propping them up on my shoulders. The new angle took me out. I lost it...orgasming hot and fast.

Denise grabbed me tighter as I collapsed on top of her, burying my face in her hair.

"So you do like me?"

"Woman, *like* is an understatement," I said, trying to catch my breath.

"But do you only like me because I'm different...than what you're used to?"

So we *weren't* past this. "Actually, yes. I do like you because you're different. You're completely different from those dried-up twigs we work with. You're completely different from anyone I've ever dated, regardless of race. I wanna know everything about you. And I've GOT to work my way in to the point where I can get you to play those drums naked."

"Shiiit, we can do that tonight," Denise said with a wink.

I pulled her sheet up over me. "Ohhhh, I am in so much trouble."

Denise laughed and scooted out of the bed. "Want some tacos first?"

"Fuck yeah, I do," I said. This just might be the woman of my dreams.

Chapter 11

The Pleasures of Being Daddy

by Henry Matthers

I couldn't believe it had taken over a year to get through this fucking divorce. I'd spent half the time regretting being the one to ask for the divorce I know we both wanted and the other half wishing I'd asked for it years ago.

What was it with the men in my family? I loved my mother dearly, but she and my father were not a good match and had never been. Nevertheless, they had raised five children together and remained married for over 50 years. The only people that seemed unaware of what a horrible match they were for each other were them.

My brothers were no different. They were all married to women that they were no longer or maybe had never been attracted to. They were all serial cheaters and seemed content to carry on that way.

I didn't want that for my life and never did. I had felt so lucky when Paula and I had met in college. She was a sweet, ambitious girl who didn't have much growing up. I didn't think my family had much either, but the way growing up with less had manifested in both of our personalities was like night and day.

I had worked hard in a field that I was passionate about and did okay for myself and my family. Or so I thought. Paula had worked her way up the corporate ladder, specializing in marketing and advertising and had been very smart about which clients she represented. She was now one of the most sought after ad-execs in the business and had become more concerned with appearances and which schools the kids went to and who they should be friends with and what parties they should attend than I could've ever believed possible.

One of my last straws had been at a dinner party with four of her miserable friends. Two couples. All high-power C level executives. I had never felt intimidated before and saw no reason to. That seemed to confound or infuriate Paula. I wasn't sure which one.

"Don't be worried about the conversation. It may be stuff that's over your head, but that's just how they are."

"Paula, I have a doctorate in education. There aren't a *lot* of things that are going to be over my head."

"Oh, Cliff. Don't start getting defensive," Paula had said, rolling her eyes as she put her earrings on. "All I'm saying is that these dinner parties are where a lot of corporate speak is done. Where deals are made. How do you think I scored—"

"Madison Kimberly. Yes, I know the story," I had told her. Of course, I knew how she had scored the hottest actress in America at the time. I had heard the story at least a dozen times.

Paula's ambition wasn't the thing that killed my love for her. It was the slow death of the person that I knew. She had gone from admiring my intellect and believing that my job shaping the minds of tomorrow was honorable work to being embarrassed that I was 'just a teacher.'

At that fateful dinner party, Paula had inconspicuously left me alone in the fancy library with her best friend's husband. He had offered me a job, telling me I could start off in an entry level role, but that he'd have me pulling at least six figures in less than a year. But not to worry because entry-level at his company was way more than I could possibly be making as a teacher.

I didn't know if I was more pissed that Paula was dissatisfied with my career and invariably my income or the fact that she had gone to her friends for help.

I wanted out. The kids were grown, and the woman I married was long gone. Paula was unrecognizable to me. When I turned down the job and gave our *friend* a piece of my mind, she had asked for a divorce during the argument that ensued. When I laughed in her face and clapped my hands, thanking God that she had finally said something that made sense to me, she was incensed. It was probably at that moment that she decide to be as big a bitch as possible during the divorce that she had asked for.

But now that was all over. It had been one year and three months. My high blood pressure and pre-diabetes were distant memories. I lived at the gym, as it had been the only way to work off my frustrations and keep from strangling Paula. I was determined not to be the overweight, sweaty, middle-aged loser looking for love at the club. I was not going to be a cliché. Even though part of me really wanted to go for a convertible, I refused to do it. I'd keep driving my truck, get into shape, and meet and date women my age. Or at least as close to it as I could get.

Once the sale of the house went through, I got myself a condo, and I could not wait to have a new woman in it, wetting up my sheets. I signed up for Tinder.

During my first week on the site, I was blown away with the quality of women. I scrolled through, shaking my head at the fact that there was a time when I thought Paula was the best I could do. These women were incredible. There was one, in particular, that caught my eye. Barbara. Barbara was 43, divorced, sexy as hell, and a seemingly good match. We chatted for a day and a half and then decided to meet in person.

Barbara didn't live far from me, so we decided to meet at the bar on the ground floor of my building for happy hour. She'd stop by on her way home from work.

I had been to the bar a few times, and I really liked it. It was small and cozy, with a fireplace, great drinks, and the best mini crab cakes I'd ever had. I hadn't dated in decades, but I felt like this was a bar that women would love.

After work, I spruced up a bit. Shaved my head, cleaned up my beard, and applied the cologne my son had instructed me to wear for my first post-divorce date.

I went down to Star Bar twenty minutes early. I wanted to have a drink to calm my nerves. Barbara had seemed really cool on the phone, but my boys had told me enough Tinder horror stories to make me second guess my app of choice.

I found a quiet table in the corner, close to the fireplace, but not too close. Chelsea, the young waitress who worked most nights, came over to take my order. I told her that I really wanted to impress this woman and that this was also somewhat of a celebratory night for me. I admitted that it was my first date since my divorce had been finalized.

"Oh, well I guess congrats are in order," she said. "Look, my boss has been trying to get rid of these bottles of Cristal left over from a party. I could bring you one half off."

"Cristal? Isn't that what the rappers drink?"

"Nope, not anymore. Now it's guys like you, Daddy."

"Okay..." I said, slightly thrown off. "Well, do you think it'll impress my date?"

"Absolutely."

"Then bring it on," I said, clapping my hands together.

Chelsea laughed at me and shook her head as she went to retrieve my champagne.

I had ten minutes until Barbara showed up. For some reason, I had assumed she would beat me here and be chilling in a corner somewhere, waiting to size me up.

Chelsea brought out the champagne and arranged it in a bucket of ice for me, placing two flutes on the table.

"Can't wait to see the woman that inspired you to spend this much on champagne," she said with a little hint of sadness.

"Between you and me, Chelsea, it's not about the woman. It's about the fact that I am free of... well, my ex-wife. Let's just say that I'm happier about that than I can fully express."

"Well, so am I, then. Since it brought you to this building and this bar. Guess I'm a pretty lucky girl."

I looked at Chelsea, really seeing her for the first time. She was a beautiful girl. Stunning, really. Long, lean, and tatted up with long dark hair and dark eyes. She couldn't be any older than my kids. Which is why I hadn't paid attention to her. I didn't want to be that guy, and I couldn't imagine what we'd have to talk about.

"Hey, good luck with your date. She's a very lucky woman," Chelsea said before she left to tend to another table.

Twenty minutes later, I got the distinct feeling that Barbara might not be coming. I looked at the fucking bottle of Cristal chilling as my phone dinged.

> Barbara: I'm soooo sorry, but I suffer from debilitating anxiety and the meds aren't quite doing the job today. This was a mistake. I still love Jim. I can't do this. SORRY!!!

Debilitating anxiety? Meds? JIM?? I didn't even know what to think about this cancellation. I didn't know whether to feel embarrassed that I had evidently been stood up or feel good that I had possibly dodged a bullet.

I noticed Chelsea looking at me sadly. Then she walked over. "What time is she supposed to be here?"

"She's not coming," I told her. "She appears to be insane."

"Oh, I see. So dating is no better for your generation than mine, I guess."

"I can't speak to that," I said, looking at my Cristal dejectedly.

Chelsea took off her apron and sat down across from me. "You know, I got off like 10 minutes ago, and I love Cristal, Daddy."

"Did you call me... Daddy?" I said laughing.

"I did...Daddy."

"Fuck. Why do I like that so much?" I said, more to myself than Chelsea.

"Would you like me to open your bottle for you?"

"No, let me get it," I said, standing up. "Are you allowed to fraternize with customers?"

"It was my boss's idea," Chelsea said, waving to another young woman across the room. "We've both had a crush on you since you moved into the building."

"A crush? On me? I must be old enough to be your father."

"Exactly. That's just what I like," Chelsea said, seductively pushing her champagne flute toward me.

I filled her glass and then mine, and before I knew it, we'd laughed and flirted our way through the entire bottle.

"Wanna go upstairs?" Chelsea asked abruptly.

"Um, yes! Yes, I do. Do you?"

"What do you think?" Chelsea said, uncrossing her legs and giving me a glimpse of hot pink under her skirt.

I stood up and led the way. I had vowed not to be the 50-something guy hooking up with a woman half his age, but I currently gave no fucks about that pledge at the moment.

No sooner had I unlocked my door than Chelsea was on me. We kissed in the doorway until Ms. Clark came out of her apartment next door. I saw the quickest flash of disappointment in her eyes.

"Oh" was all she uttered before hurrying to the elevator. She had made her intentions known several times, and I was sure she would now think that I had ignored her advances because I was into 20-year-old waitresses.

Chelsea and I laughed as we made our way into my apartment and to the living room couch.

We continued to kiss and grope each other, and I was happy to know that I didn't feel like an awkward old man at all. I wanted to fuck the shit out of this girl.

"Oooh, Daddy. I feel that hard dick. What you gonna do with it?" Chelsea said as she massaged my crotch and licked her lips.

"How about you suck Daddy's cock?"

"Mmmm, I thought you'd never ask," Chelsea said before grabbing a throw pillow and positioning herself on the floor between my legs. I probably broke a speed record unbuckling my belt and jeans and tried not to think of the fact that I used to have to beg for a blow job.

Once my pants were removed, Chelsea wasted no time. She started with the tip, licking around, teasing me. I felt all blood immediately leave my brain.

Chelsea dragged her tongue along my shaft and then was down at my balls. I honestly couldn't remember the last time anyone other than me had touched my balls.

Chelsea's tongue seemed to have a mind of its own. She spread my legs wider, and I laid my head back to allow myself to enjoy the moment.

I felt her tongue get close to my ass, and I tried not to flinch. This was a new sensation for me. I made a mental note that I liked it.

Chelsea grabbed my dick and somehow used both of her hands to twist it while sliding me into her mouth at the same time. I opened my eyes to watch her. Her eyes were closed, and she seemed to be into it.

I realized I didn't care if she was or not. She had me fooled, and that was good enough for me.

"Fuck. You taste so good, Daddy," she said before she deep-throated me.

I gripped the cushions on either side of me. It was all I could do not to grab Chelsea's head and slam into her. She felt amazing. I had not been sucked off in years. I couldn't believe I had gone this long.

Just as I felt like I was at my limit, Chelsea pulled away and stood up. She smiled at me as she took her dress off. She was standing there in just the hot pink thong, and I smiled admiringly. She was a sight. A perfect, blemish-free body stood in front of me, and I just wanted to kiss and suck every part of it. I felt momentary guilt because my ex-wife had carried and delivered my three children. There was a time that I loved every stretch mark and bulge on her body, but those days were long gone.

Chelsea slid off her pink thong and walked over to me. She had a little patch of hair between her legs that just looked delectable.

"Daddy...I wanna know what that dick do," Chelsea said before straddling me. She grabbed my dick like it belonged to her and squeezed it as she put it inside of her.

I threw my head back and closed my eyes as I held on to Chelsea's slim hips. She did some kind of move where she'd pause right at the tip of my dick and then slide down.

"Shit, Daddy. I knew you would have good dick. Some crazy bitch let *this* go," she said hoarsely.

"I'm sorry. No disrespect, but you are a fucking catch. God, you feel so good," Chelsea continued, stroking my ego in ways she couldn't know. "You're so fucking hard, Daddy. You're about to make me wash this dick."

I opened my eyes to take in the sight of this beautiful woman riding my dick like it was the best thing she'd felt in her life. I felt her tighten around me as she grabbed my shoulders and threw her head back.

"Fuck yes, Ohhhh. I needed that. Yes!"

As I felt Chelsea's wetness spread over my thighs, it was my turn. I grabbed her hips and pumped into her as fast as I could until I felt myself explode inside of her. I felt all the pent-up frustration of the last few months leave my body and laughed to myself as I agreed with Chelsea.

"Fuck, I needed that too. I don't think I knew how bad."

Chelsea climbed off of me and went to the bathroom while I grabbed a bottle of Tanqueray and made us a couple of gin and tonics.

Chelsea came out of the bathroom, and I admired her tatted-up body once again as she laughed and told me that her dad drank Tanqueray.

"Let's take our drinks out on the balcony," Chelsea said. "Do you have a comforter?"

I pointed to the linen closet as I wiped off the counter, and Chelsea grabbed two thick blankets. She wrapped herself in one and went out to the balcony. I asked no questions and wrapped myself in the other before meeting her out there with our drinks. She had pushed the chairs over in the corner and was sitting on the ground. I had to admit that I had never even sat out there at all. The view was stunning as the sun was just about down. I closed the door behind me and joined her on the ground. I felt like twelve-year-old me at a campout.

As we sipped our drinks, Chelsea turned to face me. She reached into my blanket and grabbed my dick, which just happened to be coming alive again.

"Mmmm," she said. "Daddy's ready for more."

She lay back, covering herself strategically while opening her legs, beckoning me. I refused to allow myself to feel the nervousness, wondering if anyone could see us, because suddenly, I didn't care. I pulled my blanket around my shoulders and climbed on top of beautiful Chelsea.

"Take this pussy, Daddy. It's yours."

And I did. All night long.

Conclusion

Hello again friends,

I hope you enjoyed this book of sexy, steamy erotica. It's an absolute highlight of my year putting it together for you.

If you're a fan, be sure to check out my other books and audiobooks. You will not be disappointed.

And one more thing. I would be so appreciative if you would leave a review. It only takes a few seconds, and it really helps people find the book.

Thank you so much. Until next time!

XOXO,

Rayna

www.ingramcontent.com/pod-product-compliance
Lightning Source LLC
Chambersburg PA
CBHW060449310726
48977CB00001B/373